THE BETTER MOTHER

EMILY SHINER

INKUBATOR
BOOKS

Published by Inkubator Books
www.inkubatorbooks.com

Copyright © 2023 by Emily Shiner

Emily Shiner has asserted her right to be identified as the author of this work.

ISBN (eBook): 978-1-83756-226-8
ISBN (Paperback): 978-1-83756-227-5
ISBN (Hardback): 978-1-83756-228-2

1

ZOE

Sunday March 5

The phone only rings once. Once and it pulls me from my sleep, yanking me out of a wonderful dream where I was on the beach in a bikini, my husband walking towards me, two drinks with cute little umbrellas in his hands. One ring and I feel like I'm pulled from my dream, yanked up and out of it, and I sit up, covers falling down around my waist, reaching over to wake him up in case he didn't hear it.

But he did. Of course he did. He's even more trained than I am to the sound of the phone and I wouldn't be surprised if he *felt* it about to ring before it made a sound. Who knows why someone might be calling this time of night?

An emergency. Gunshot wound, maybe?

Some problem with a patient he operated on earlier in the day?

A nurse with questions that could easily be answered by someone else?

That last one, that's the one that really makes him mad. And a nurse might call once with a silly question, but only once, because Ethan will make sure she learns her lesson not to call at two in the morning when she should learn how to read the chart correctly.

I blink at the clock. The numbers are too fuzzy for me to read.

"This is Dr. Steele." There's a pause as he listens to whoever is talking.

I roll over and pull the blankets up over my head so the glow from his phone doesn't shine into my eyes. It's not very bright, not in the grand scheme of things, but right now it feels like someone is shining a searchlight right into my face.

"Who is this?"

There's an edge to his voice and I feel a dash of pity for whatever nurse was stupid enough to call him right now. Shifting, I twist my arm so my Fitbit lights up. 3:30 a.m. Oof, whoever's on the other end of that phone call is about to see how unpleasant my husband can be.

"Why are you calling me?"

I'm pretty sure that's what he said, anyway. It's hard to hear with the blankets up around my ears and I shift some, poking my head out a bit while keeping my eyes squeezed shut. This isn't how the script usually goes when a nurse calls him. They usually identify themselves and explain why they woke him up right off the bat.

Maybe his reputation precedes him and they don't want to tell him who they are.

I chuckle. That's what they get for waking him up.

"I don't know how you got this number or what you

want." The bed rocks as he throws his covers over onto my side and swings his legs out to stand. A slight pause, like the person is talking, trying to backtrack what's going on. "How did you get this number?"

Now I'm fully invested and even though I know I'm going to have a hard time getting back to sleep, I want to see this through and find out what's going on.

The bathroom light clicks on and Ethan closes the door, muffling his voice. Then he turns on the exhaust, making it impossible for me to hear anything else that's being said.

What's that about? I start to get out of bed, then I stop. If it's a work problem—and it has to be a work problem, right?—then I doubt Ethan will want me to know anything about it. He likes to keep his work and personal lives separate—or as separate as you can when you're a surgeon and you constantly get calls at home.

But I'm still curious. Still, the bed is nice and warm, the floor is going to be cold if I step on it in bare feet, and Ethan will tell me what's going on when he comes back to bed. I know about HIPPA and the importance of doctor-patient privacy, but let's get real.

The stories are just too good. They never go farther than my ears, of course, but they're fun to hear and think about. If something crazy is going on with a patient or one of his nurses, he'll tell me. It might not happen tonight, not when we both need more sleep than we've gotten, but I'm sure I'll hear about it at breakfast.

Satisfied, I roll over and pull the blankets up around my shoulders as I wait for him to come back to bed.

Luckily, I don't have long to wait. I hear the bathroom exhaust turn off and see the way the room lightens some as he opens the bathroom door before he flicks the light switch.

Then he uses the light from his cell phone to walk back across the room before crawling into bed with me.

"What was that?" I'm sleepy and I reach out, resting my hand on his chest. He's chilled from being out from under the covers and his heart is pounding.

"Wrong number." Ethan clears his throat and rolls towards me, feeling for me in the dark. When he finds my cheek he cups it, then leans forward and gives me a kiss. "Can you believe it? At this time of night?"

"Nothing good is going on right now," I murmur. "Hopefully they'll go to bed and stop waking people up."

A wrong number. Geez. Right when I was having such an amazing dream, and with only a few more hours of sleep to go. I'll be lucky to fall back asleep within the hour, then it'll be almost time to get up and do some yoga, start breakfast, and get Anna up.

At least the phone call didn't wake her, or she'd be in full wide-awake-toddler mode.

"Go back to sleep, Zoe," Ethan whispers, and kisses me once more.

I nod, snuggling into his chest and wrapping my arms around him. His heart hammers wildly, like he's just ran a marathon. Or got some terrible news.

Wrong number.

That's what he said. He made it sound convincing.

But I don't know if I believe him.

2

ZOE

Monday March 6

"**A**nna Banana," I say, trying to keep my tone as firm and in control as possible, "you know full well that you can't go to preschool wearing only a rain jacket and your diaper."

She giggles and wraps the rain jacket tight around her body, screaming with glee as I swoop in and pick her up, tucking her under my arm like a football. Maybe it's not *technically* a professional way to carry your child through the house, but it keeps her from squirming out of my grip.

"No clothes!" She shrieks the words, hammering my back with her little fists. They bounce off harmlessly, and I grin, adjusting my grip so I can tickle her. Another shriek, and I spin her up, then pop her on my hip so I can look her in the eyes.

"No clothes means no preschool," I tell her, my voice

serious. "Then you won't get to see your friends."

"My fwends." Her lower lip wobbles.

I nod. "They want to see you. Their mommies called me this morning to tell me that, but you have to wear clothes to go see them."

She nods, her eyes wide, her mouth a tight line. If there's anything that will make Anna do what I want her to, it's telling her that she can see her friends if she plays along. She's three, and a handful, but loves her friends fiercely. Do I use that to my advantage from time to time?

Sure. What parent wouldn't?

But it's not a bad thing. She'll get to go to preschool and not only see her friends, but work on learning her letters, and I'll have time to clean up the house, run to the store, and have a hot meal on the table when Ethan gets home from work.

I felt a lot of guilt when we started sending Anna to preschool in the beginning. I'm a stay-at-home mom. Why wouldn't she stay at home with me? But then Ethan sent me some articles about child development and how it's actually good for them to be around other kids their age. They need that interaction and time to play away from parents, and I agreed. I work with her on her letters when we're at home, of course. I'm not totally hands-off.

But I have to admit that I'm a better mother than I was before, when she was at home with me all the time. I have all of the household chores done before I pick her up right before lunch and she gets all of my attention. We love to go to the park or read books or bake cookies, and it's just the two of us.

I wasn't about to put her in an all-day program, but four hours every morning has given me the free time I need to get some things done. I'm on top of it, I have time to take care of myself, and I have time to be a supportive wife.

In short, preschool is awesome.

"What is all the commotion in here?" Ethan sweeps into the room, pulling on his jacket as he does. He doesn't need to wear slacks and a suit jacket to the hospital every morning, but he says he likes the way he looks before he changes into his white coat. Professional. Put-together. In control.

"Anna here was going to bring me her shirt and pants I left on her bed," I say, putting our daughter down.

She slithers from my grasp and stares up at her dad for a moment before darting from the room.

"I told her she couldn't go to preschool dressed like that and that her friends wanted to see her today."

"Smart." Ethan kisses me, his hand on my hip, and I step into him. How many couples still feel the fire between them like we do? I know from reading books and watching TV that a lot of couples grow out of love, but not us. The more successful he is at work, the more effort he puts into our marriage. I don't know how he does it, but that's part of the reason I'm so willing to work hard around the house.

We support each other. It all works out.

"You hungry? I made French toast and have a fruit salad I put together while you were shaving." I gesture to the loaded table behind me. Anna only finished half of her food and I'm not surprised when Ethan picks up her plate and takes a bite.

"This is enough, thanks. There are some drug reps coming by this morning and they always bring a huge spread of food to try to woo us. I don't want to miss out on whatever muffins they bring." He pops a strawberry into his mouth and grins.

"It must be so hard being a doctor," I tease. "All the free food. The nice car. The phone calls in the middle of the night." I turn to look at him as I speak and I see the shadow that crosses his face.

There and gone. Ethan is unflappable.

"I hate wrong numbers more than nurses who ask stupid questions," he tells me. "Were you able to get back to sleep?"

Something about it being a *wrong number* doesn't sit right with me. But if I push it with him then I risk derailing the entire morning, and I know how much Ethan hates arguing before surgery. He says it throws him off his game.

"I was," I say, and it's only a bit of a lie. When I'm up in the night it takes me a long time to pass back out, but I managed to get another hour or so before my Fitbit buzzed to wake me. That silent alarm lets me slip from bed without accidentally jostling Ethan, although he's often up around the same time, lacing up his shoes to go for a run.

"Well, I'm glad. I'm sorry again about last night. I couldn't hear what they were saying and I thought it was someone from the hospital." He sighs and puts Anna's plate back down on the table. "Hopefully tonight we'll get better sleep. Hey, what about a nap? Anna still takes them, so why don't you take one too?"

"I might," I admit. Even though it's early and caffeine is working its way through my veins, I already feel a little tired. Even a little catnap, just enough to help clear the cobwebs from my mind, would be great. "Do you have surgery this afternoon? I was thinking about making chicken cordon bleu for dinner but I wanted to make sure you were going to be home."

"My favorite," he tells me, pouring coffee into his travel mug before swirling in some cream and stirring in sugar. He groans. "Wait. I forgot. I have a dinner I have to go to, and I don't think it's optional."

I feel my heart sink. It's inappropriate, right, to get upset like that because your husband has something else to do? But I genuinely like spending time with Ethan. When I got pregnant with Anna and stopped working I lost some of my friends. I know relying on your spouse to fill that gap for you isn't the smartest move, but Ethan stepped into the role effortlessly.

I smile. "Not a problem, I can move tonight's dinner to tomorrow. Tonight Anna and I will have mac-and-cheese from the blue box and watch cartoons before she goes to bed."

Ethan laughs. "You make it look good, you know that?"

"What?"

"Being a mother. Some women don't make it look easy or fun, but you do. I'm in awe of you, Zoe Steele."

"I'm in awe of you," I tell him. "What's the dinner tonight?"

"You're asking what in the world could possibly be better than macaroni with my family?" Ethan waits as I laugh and nod, then continues. "Some of the other docs wanted to get together outside of the hospital cafeteria and have dinner. I don't think there's any dark motive to it. Dinner with the docs."

"Sounds thrilling." Personally, I'd rather be home with Anna. Yes, sometimes I miss going out and being Ethan's date to various dinners, but if they're just going downtown to grab a bite to eat, I'm perfectly content staying behind. I could get all dressed up and squeeze into a dress and heels, or I can stay here and put on some sweats and hang out with my favorite girl.

Easy decision.

He looks like he's about to say something else, but then Anna streaks back into the kitchen. She's left the rain jacket in her bedroom, thank goodness, but she's stepped into her shirt, and has her arms through the legs of her pants. I bend down and catch her right as she tries to barrel past me.

"You've got your hands full," Ethan remarks, walking over and giving me a kiss. "You're the best mom, Zoe." He leans down and plants a kiss on the top of Anna's hair. "Try to be good for your mom, kiddo. She deserves a gold star."

"I love you," I tell him. Anna's fast, but I'm faster, and I get the pants yanked off her arms before she has time to complain. "Text me. I'll see you tonight."

"I can't wait. If something comes up, I'll let you know."

He's gone then, and just like that, it feels quieter in the house. Ethan isn't a loud guy, not by any means, but still, when he leaves, everything gets quieter. That's who he is and why he's so popular. Not only is he a great surgeon, but he's driven and focused and has this way of talking to people that makes them feel like they're the only ones on the planet.

Everyone loves him.

"Okay, girlie," I say, kneeling down to help Anna with her clothes. "You are going to have a wonderful morning at preschool and I'm going to run some errands. Then tonight, it's you and me."

"You and me!" Anna squeals and throws her little arms around my neck. I stop trying to wrestle her into her clothes and hug her back.

Her and me. I wish Ethan were coming home for dinner tonight, but we'll make the best of it. Our family is wonderful. Perfect. Nothing can change that.

3

MICAH

Monday March 13

"Mom?" I already know she's not going to answer me but I still lean my head into her bedroom and call out for her, keeping my voice low on the off-chance she's sleeping off a hangover.

No answer.

The door creaks when I push it open. I walk into her room and reach for the light switch before remembering that the power was turned off yesterday. This happens from time to time. She goes out drinking or takes too many drugs and then the power gets turned off, but it always gets turned back on eventually.

But she's been gone a week. The power has been off for a day. I don't know much about paying bills, but I'm sure there's a fee to get it turned back on. For that to happen, though, Mom has to show up. She has to have some money.

She has to not have shot it into her arm or snorted it up her nose.

"Mom, I'm hungry." I walk over to her bed and prod the pile of blankets, hoping that she's there. For a moment I think about what it would be like to find her body here, to poke her and have her not move, but I push that thought from my mind. She's not here. Her body isn't under this pile.

Sighing, I turn and sit on the edge of her bed. The mattress sags and a spring pops up into my thigh. Everything here is falling apart, everything is old and damaged and stained and dirty.

My mind drifts to my laptop. I won it last summer when I wrote an essay about the effects of pollution on the town's greenways. Mom hadn't helped me. She hadn't even known that I was working on a paper. It was Mrs. Caldwell down at the library who encouraged me to write it and helped me turn it in. She even paid for me to print it off at the library because we don't have a printer.

We didn't have a computer then, but I do now. Mom doesn't know. I keep it under my bed when I'm not using it and I only log onto the neighbor's Wi-Fi. That's how I know what to do now. I have a plan.

"Mom, I'm not going to stick around and wait for you." I pause in the door of her bedroom, fully aware that she's not here, that she can't hear me. Still, I want to tell her how bad it hurts when she disappears like this. I want her to know that it breaks my heart that she's not a great mom. "I'm leaving. I don't know when you'll be back. I don't know when I'll be back. If I'll come back."

I pause, my fingers on her doorknob, then I pull her door closed behind me. It only takes a few minutes in my room to pack up my backpack. I have the notebook I need for school with me, but all of my books are in my locker. I grab my toothbrush but leave the little tube of toothpaste I received in a care package from the school.

When she gets back she'll need that. I'll be fine without it.

I glance in my closet but turn away from the clothes stuffed in there on a shelf. They're old, and dirty, and embarrassing. Nothing I have in there is worth taking with me to my new life.

At the last second I drop to my knees and grab my laptop from under my bed. I've done everything possible to keep it hidden from my mom. How was I to know if she would let me keep it or if she would try to sell it? She sold everything in the house that she could to get some extra money. The last thing I wanted was to lose my laptop after I worked so hard to get it.

It's sleek, sleeker than most laptops kids my age have. Even if it weren't a nice once, I wouldn't care, because it's mine and it works and I carefully wrap a hoodie around it before sliding it into my backpack.

At the front door I pause. Do I lock the door?

Mom doesn't always take a key with her. She likes me to let her back in when she gets home.

"You know what, Mom? I'm tired of always taking care of you. I want someone else to take care of me for once." My backpack strap digs into my shoulder and I adjust it as I stand on the front porch. Finally, I slip my house key from my pocket and lock the door.

"There. I can't do it all for you. I'm done." My voice cracks and I tuck the key back in my pocket, hitching my backpack higher once again as I turn away from the front door. I have enough money for a taxi so I don't have to walk all the way across town. I dig the cash out of my pocket and turn once to look back at the house before starting the walk to the library.

I don't have a phone but Mrs. Caldwell will let me call from the library. I know she will. I won't tell her that Mom is missing, just like I haven't told her when it's happened before. All I need is to make a call. Get a taxi.

Change my life.

4

ZOE

"Well, you had to wait a week for the chicken cordon bleu, but I promise you it will have been worth it." I cradle my cell between my cheek and my shoulder as I open the oven to look inside. Steam and a delicious smell waft out and I inhale before closing the door and turning off the oven. "Are you leaving the hospital now?"

"About to pull into the driveway, actually." Ethan sounds amused, like he pulled one over on me. "I didn't have any patients to check up on this afternoon so I finished some charts and came home a bit early. Hope that's not a problem."

"It's great." I grin, then cover the receiver with my hand. "Anna! Your dad's home!"

"See you, Zoe." Ethan hangs up before I can respond. Behind me, I hear Anna open the door to the garage.

"Wait for Daddy to pull in," I call out, glancing over my shoulder before bending back down to get the chicken out of the oven. Anna's a good kid. Three is a lot more fun than two was and I feel like I can actually reason a bit with her rather than having her throw fits when she doesn't like something.

And yes, I know things might get worse again. And then she'll be a teenager, but we have a long time to wait for that to happen, thank goodness.

I'm putting the chicken and roasted potatoes on a serving platter when Ethan sweeps into the kitchen, Anna on his hip. He has a bunch of flowers in his hand and moves to hand them to me, but then sees I'm busy. Instead of dropping them on the counter, he plops Anna on the counter, then grabs a vase from the cabinet above the sink. In a moment the two of them are arranging a beautiful display.

"What are those for?" I wipe my hands on my apron and give my husband a kiss, noting with pleasure how he puts a hand on Anna's shoulder to steady her before looking away from her. He's so careful. Has such good attention to detail.

"I missed you today. It's been a busy day and I missed you. It's not fair that I have to be away from you sometimes."

"You're saving lives. Doing what you've always wanted to do." It's what I always say whenever people comment on how much Ethan works. I knew, when I got pregnant and quit my job as a nurse, that I wouldn't get to see him nearly as much as I wanted, but there wasn't any way I would ask him to stay home. Number one, he'd go insane not at the hospital in the thick of it.

Number two is that he loves taking care of his patients.

And finally, selfishly, I wouldn't want to give up my time with Anna. Sure, we miss him when he has to work late and we're snuggled up to eat mac-and-cheese and watch cartoons, but I'll always treasure that time with my daughter.

"Yes, but I still miss you." He adjusts a rose and then hands me the flowers to put on the table before helping

Anna get down from the counter. "I don't like working late. I don't like the meetings I have to go to. I want to be here with you."

He pouts and I laugh, pulling him to me for a kiss.

"Well, one of us has to pay to keep the lights on in this place, buddy," I say, running my fingers through his hair. It's thick and dark, with a bit of a wave to it. I always thought he looked like a movie star. Anna has his hair, the lucky thing. Mine is blonde and so straight it can't hold a curl to save my life.

"I'm thrilled to do that for us," he tells me, his voice lower. "I miss you."

I lean into him to kiss him but Anna pushes between us. "Hungry!" She squeals the word and both Ethan and I wince.

"Sorry," I say, grabbing our daughter and helping her into her high chair. "We didn't want to have big snacks this afternoon so we could enjoy a meal with you."

"Not a problem. Maybe there can be some alone time later." Ethan winks at me over Anna's head while I serve us. In addition to the chicken and potatoes I made a kale salad with a goat cheese dressing and artichoke hearts. Fresh cookies that Anna helped bake are cooling on the counter.

"I don't see why not." I flip Anna's napkin onto her lap and then sit back in my seat. "Anna's already had her bath, so she'll be ready to head to bed as soon as dinner is over. Maybe we pop on a movie, like we're in high school?"

He laughs and takes a bite of his chicken. "If only I'd known you in high school I don't think I would have had trouble gaining weight to make the football team."

"Sure, but then you might have broken your nose or something. You wouldn't be a model."

He laughs and I stab my fork through the air at him. "I'm serious, Ethan. Have you looked in a mirror lately? It's a good thing you wear your ring at work or I'd have to worry about women following you home when you weren't paying attention."

He laughs again and shakes his head, but he doesn't know I'm serious. Ethan is devastatingly good looking. Anna's lucky that she takes after him, although I do feel a little bad for all the hearts she's going to break when she's older.

I fight to clear the thought. She's three, for goodness' sake, so it's not like I'm going to have to worry about that anytime soon.

"Everything alright?" Ethan's staring at me, his fork halfway to his mouth. Between us, Anna shovels potatoes in her mouth like it's her job.

"Yeah, I'm thinking about what it will be like when Anna's older." I reach over and ruffle our daughter's hair. "I wonder if I'll go back to work."

"Are you feeling the empty nest syndrome already?" He chuckles. "You know I fully support you to do whatever you want when she's in school. You want to come work at the hospital some more? You should. Or maybe start really working on your calligraphy. You've talked before about starting a little business."

"Maybe," I say, trying to sound nonchalant. Inside, though, I'm burning with pleasure. He's such a good listener. Even if he isn't particularly interested in what I'm doing, he always makes sure I get the support I need to feel like I can tackle anything that comes my way. I know how lucky I am.

"You'll come up with what you want to do. And maybe that's staying home and eating ice cream while watching soaps." Ethan stands and gestures to the kitchen. "You want some wine? I think a glass of white would go perfectly with this."

"No, thanks, but go for it. I think there's some Riesling open on the top shelf, but don't feel like you have to have that if you want something else."

He leaves and I watch Anna eat for a moment before the doorbell rings. I start, then toss my napkin on the table. "I've got it," I call to Ethan, then drop a kiss on Anna's head.

Even without having any wine with dinner, I feel like I'm buzzing slightly as I walk down the hall to the front door. That's what being in love with Ethan does to me—it makes me feel like I'm floating, like I'm walking with my head in the clouds. I love that about him, love the way we both bring out the best in each other.

The doorbell rings again.

"I'm coming!" Hurrying now, I rush down the hall to the front door. I'd thought at first maybe it was a late Amazon delivery. Ethan is always ordering stuff between patients and it's fun to see what gets delivered the next day. But they don't normally ring the bell.

And they certainly don't ring it twice.

There's a knock on the door as I fumble for the lock and throw it, finally swinging the door open to see who's so eager to get our attention. "I'm coming," I say, plastering a smile on my face as I look out onto the porch.

There's a boy there. Young. With thick dark hair falling down on his forehead and a serious expression on his face. "Hi," he says, shifting his backpack higher on his shoulder as he lifts his hand in a wave.

I grip the doorframe, trying to steady myself. Before, I felt tipsy, like everything was exciting. Life was bubbly. Now I suddenly feel heavy, my stomach falling through to my feet, my mouth dropping open as I take in the boy on the front porch.

I've never seen him before, but that doesn't matter. I still know exactly who he is. Who he has to be.

There's no way he can be anyone but my husband's son.

5

ZOE

"Who's there?" Ethan's voice, as well as how unconcerned he sounds, makes me look back over my shoulder. He's coming down the hall, a glass of wine in his hand. From the kitchen I can hear Anna talking to herself.

It's like time stands still. I'm suddenly and acutely aware that no matter what I do for the rest of my life, I'll remember this moment in time. There won't be any way for me to forget it, to forget every single detail of it. Even when I'm on my deathbed, I'm sure I'll be able to conjure up the memory of the way the wind blows past the boy towards me, the smell of him slightly sour and unshowered.

I'll remember how my dinner feels heavy in my stomach, like I'm going to be sick, and the overbearing knowledge that as soon as Ethan looks out the door and sees who's on our porch, everything will change.

I'm suddenly struck with the terrible thought that I need to close the door, lock it, walk away from it. That maybe this is a nightmare and maybe—if I could only pull myself together long enough to do it—I could close the door and undo whatever is about to happen.

But instead I step to the side, my hand still on the door, my eyes locked on the boy.

"Someone's here to see you," I manage, but my voice sounds strangled. I don't know if Ethan hears the strange tone in my voice because I can't tear my eyes away from the boy long enough to look at my husband. I feel him next to me, smell the slightly antiseptic scent he always brings with him from the hospital, then it feels like the earth tilts on its axis, hard, and when it tilts back, everything is different.

"Hello." The boy scuffs his toe against our welcome mat. His shoes are worn, dirty. They look too small, like his feet are about to pop from how squeezed they are. I drag my eyes up him, taking in the fact that his pants are too short, his shirt is stained, his eyes are wide and haunted. "I think you're my dad."

There it is. I exhale hard, in a whoosh, and lean back against Ethan. His hand is immediately on my hip, his fingers digging through my clothes like he's trying to pin me in place, trying to keep me here with him.

"What's your name?" Ethan sounds strangely in control. Detached.

I risk a glance back at him, curious what he looks like. Is this how he acts with patients when he knows the worst and he has to tell them their time is limited? Is this a glimpse into how he separates himself from the truth so he doesn't fall apart every time he has to give bad news?

"I'm Micah." The boy scuffs the mat again. "My mom told me you were my dad."

Silence. I can't breathe.

"Who's your mom?"

I stare at the boy, willing him to say a name my husband has never heard. As I wait, I wrack my brain, trying to think of all the names of the exes he's told me over the years. Rather than helping me right now, though, my brain is a traitor. I can't think of anything beyond what's happening right now.

"Rita. You two dated when you were in college." The boy glances at me, an apology on his face, then looks back at Ethan.

I want to look at Ethan but I can't tear my eyes away from the boy.

And I don't want to see it. The truth is there in the set of his jaw. The way his nostrils flare a bit. I see it in the tip of his ear, the way he clenches his hand into a fist before forcing himself to relax.

This boy is my husband's son. Anyone could see it.

"Rita." The way my husband says this other woman's name makes me turn to him.

"You know her?"

His jaw tightens before he speaks. "I know her. *Knew* her, actually. We dated a little while in college but then broke up. I never saw her again." He sighs and runs his hand through his hair, pushing it back from his face. "Where's your mom?"

The boy's eyes widen.

"Hey, Micah. I'm Zoe." I take a deep breath. "It's going to be fine. You're fine, I promise," I add, hoping to try to take the edge off what's going on.

The boy glances at me. "She's been gone a week," he says, his voice soft. Then he looks back at Ethan. "I don't know where she went. She runs off sometimes, leaves me at home. Usually she's back by now but this time, she didn't come back. I didn't know what to do. I hope she's okay, but maybe she's hurt? Or... or dead." He swallows hard. "There's no power at the house, no food..." His voice trails off.

"We're eating dinner," I say, finally stepping away from Ethan and reaching out for the boy. My hand falls before I touch his arm. "Why don't you come on in and get something to eat? The three of us can talk things through. Maybe we can help you find your mom."

He nods, then shrugs. "When she disappears like this, she doesn't want to be found. She wants to... do whatever she wants."

I exhale hard and turn to Ethan, searching his face for any help. He looks shocked, like any man would in this situation. I don't know how to take control of this, or what the right thing to do is, but I do know I can't leave this boy—leave Micah—out here on the porch. "Come on in, Micah. You're welcome to eat with us while we figure this all out."

The boy shrugs again before brushing past me into the hall.

I gesture to Ethan to follow him. "Show him where to go," I say, my voice low so Micah won't hear me. "Make sure he washes his hands."

"Are you sure we shouldn't call the police?" Ethan's voice is as low as mine, but he glances over his shoulder to ensure Micah isn't listening.

He isn't. His head is on a swivel taking in all of our family photos in the hall as he walks away from us. I stare at his back for a moment before looking back at Ethan and shaking my head.

"We will," I say, "but not yet. Right now we need to feed this poor kid and find out what's going on." I pause, not wanting to ask the question on my lips but also knowing there's no way for us to move forward without me doing exactly that. "Ethan, do you think...?" My voice trails off.

He grabs my hand, still holding his wine with the other. I stare at it for a moment before forcing myself to look up at him. "Zoe, I promise you, Rita was before you. That boy... he has to be a teenager. I never knew about him, I swear."

I believe him. There's still one more question I have to ask, even though I know the answer.

"But you think he's yours?"

"Zoe, I can't imagine that he's not. Look at him." Ethan squeezes my hand. "I'm sorry," he says, and his voice breaks. "I had no idea, I promise you that. But there's no way that Micah isn't mine."

He lets go of my hand and turns away to follow Micah down the hall to the kitchen. I should follow them. I should make sure Micah does a good job washing his hands, should make sure Anna isn't going to act out when she sees that we have a visitor.

Her brother.

No, I can't think like that. Turning, I close the front door and carefully lock it, the thunk of the lock loud as it slips into place.

I lean against the front door. My legs are weak and I give in, sliding down it until I'm sitting on the floor.

In the kitchen, I hear Anna laughing. I hear Ethan's low voice, then Micah's.

My husband's son just showed up at my house.

And I invited him in.

I hope I didn't make a huge mistake.

6

MICAH

It's embarrassing to stand at the sink and wash my hands while my dad looks on. I don't remember the last time my mom bought hand soap, so I've been using this body wash that I stole from the gym. Someone brought some name-brand stuff and then left the bottle after their shower. It was only half-full, but I nicked it anyway.

I'd been using it to wash everything. Myself, my hair, my hands. Dishes. Clothes. In the sink, of course, because mom sold our washing machine a while ago to try to make some quick cash. I don't know much about appliances, but I do know you should be able to get more than fifty bucks for something like that.

But my body wash ran out a few days ago. I know I smell. I see the way kids look at me when I get on the bus, like they'd rather be anywhere in the world than sharing a seat with me, and while I hate them for it, I don't blame them.

I don't want to share a seat with me. And I'm me.

Dirt swirls around the drain. The sink is deep, bright white. I hate the way the dirt settles in the bottom and I use my hands to splash some water around to try to rinse it all the way out.

"Don't worry about it." That's my dad. He's holding a towel out to me.

I take it, still nervous that I'm not quite clean. The towel is white and fluffy and soft and I don't want to make it dirty, but I dry my hands anyway, then hand it back.

He takes it from me and turns to hang it on the oven.

While his back is to me, I get to look around without having him watch me check everything out. This kitchen is huge. There's enough room for a table, and I glance at that for a moment before letting my eyes drag over the rest of the space. Bright white tile on the floor, stainless steel appliances, even two ovens.

I don't know how I didn't see that before. Two ovens. A small refrigerator with a glass door next to them.

"What's that?" I point at the clear door.

"A wine fridge." Dad sounds wary, like he's not sure how I'm going to take the news that they have a wine fridge in their kitchen and we couldn't even keep the lights on.

I nod but don't say anything. I've seen pictures of places like this in books but I honestly never thought I'd be in one. I don't fit in, and that's made even more apparent when I walk to the table. My dad opens some cupboards behind me and I hear the sound of dishes clattering. A moment later he puts a plate and some silverware down at an empty seat and gestures me to it.

"Sit," he tells me, and I do. "I would offer you wine because you look like you need a glass, but I have a very good feeling you're too young." He slides into the seat across from me.

I nod and look at the little kid sitting to my left. I noticed her when I walked in but I hadn't wanted to look at her. She's cute, with pigtails that are droopy and falling out of their bands, and a button nose. "What's your name?" I ask.

"Anna." She stabs a bite of chicken from her plate and waves it at me before shoving it in her mouth.

"I'm Micah." I pause, trying to get my tongue to work around the words I want to say next. "I'm your brother."

There's a gasp from the kitchen door and I look up. Zoe stands there, her mouth slightly open, her hand at her throat. Immediately, I know I did something wrong, said something I shouldn't, but I can't think of what it is.

It's true, isn't it? We have the same dad. Our moms might be different, but we're still siblings. I have a little sister.

It's exciting.

Zoe walks across the kitchen to pour herself a glass of wine before turning back to the table. When she does, she's smiling, but it looks forced. "Why don't we eat?" asks Zoe, and she sits down across from Anna, next to my dad. They look like the perfect couple sitting there. "How old are you, Micah?"

My dad loads up my plate while she talks and I know I should answer her, but I'm so hungry. Before I can stop myself, I take a bite of chicken. God, it's good.

"What is this?" I ask, moving the meat over in my mouth so I can speak.

"Chicken cordon bleu." She smiles at me, but there's a bit of tension around her mouth like she's not sure what's going to happen.

I put that tension there and I immediately feel bad.

"It's delicious." I stab another bite but make myself wait before eating it. "And I'm thirteen."

She glances at my dad and I can almost see her doing the math. "Thirteen, huh? I loved being a teenager."

I nod and cram another bite of chicken in my mouth, trying to think. I want them to believe me. I *need* them to believe me. Never in my life have I wanted anything more than to be invited to this table to sit and eat dinner.

I feel safe here.

"I have a picture," I say, dropping my fork to my plate. It clatters loudly and Anna laughs, but Zoe and my dad don't blink. "Hold on." Turning, I unzip my backpack, but I don't pull out my laptop. There's a wad of clothes to push past, but then I find what I'm looking for. I don't want to pull out all of my pictures, but I do pull out one and I offer it across the table. "Here you go, Dad."

He blinks hard at that but takes it from me, turning it so he can get a better look at it. Zoe must be curious too, because she leans over, resting her hand on my dad's arm as they look at the picture together.

"It's you and mom," I say, unable to bear the silence any longer. "She told me that you two took it when you were dating."

"That's Rita." My dad's voice is soft and he hands it to Zoe to look at.

She glances at the photo and then puts it down on the table.

My fingers itch to reach out and take it back, but nothing bad is going to happen to it. They're not going to rip it up or keep it or anything. I trust them.

He's my dad.

And Zoe? She's not my mom, but she's nice. I like her.

That realization sends a shock of guilt through me. I *have* a mom. Why in the world do I care if this woman is nice or not?

Both Dad and Zoe are quiet, and I feel the need to fill the silence. "Mom gave it to me a long time ago. I thought you might want to see it, maybe to prove that I'm really who I say I am." I take another bite while I wait for a response. My stomach feels like it's eating itself, I'm so hungry.

"I believe you." Zoe rests her elbows on the table and looks at me. "Okay, Micah. You're thirteen. Your mom disappeared, but she told you about your dad before that happened, right?"

I nod. "That's right."

"And so you decided to come here when she didn't come home." She exhales hard, takes a sip of wine. "That was very brave of you, but you had to be scared."

"I was. I went to the library and they helped me call a taxi to come here. I didn't think I'd be able to find it if I walked, but I knew the address."

She takes another sip of wine. I glance over at my dad and I'm not surprised to see that he's finished his glass. "We're glad you're here and not still in your house waiting on your mom. Do you have a phone number for her? Some way we can get in touch with her?"

Stupid tears burn my eyes. I don't want them to see me cry but I can't help it. "I don't have her number. She... goes off. Does drugs. I don't know what to say." There's a sob in my throat but I hold it back. I don't want them to think I'm weak or obnoxious or a problem.

"Oh, honey, it's going to all work out." She's out of her chair and around the table before I can make another sound. "You're safe here. I want you to finish eating and we'll show you the bathroom for a shower. You have to be exhausted, so you need a good night's sleep. We'll figure this all out, I promise you."

I nod and take another bite. I'm still hungry but all this talk of my mom makes the food sit heavy in my stomach. I don't like thinking about her disappearing and what that might mean for her. At the same time, I don't like thinking about how much better my life would have been had my dad known about me in the first place.

"I think I'm ready to shower now," I say, pushing back from the table. There's a noise from next to me and I look over at Anna. She's grinning at me.

"I'll show you the bathroom." That's my dad. It's the first thing he's said in a while and I'm grateful he's the one who leads me from the kitchen.

I should thank Zoe for dinner and for letting me in the house, but I can't seem to make my mouth form any words. All I can think about is my mom. Never in my life have I wanted anything bad to happen to her, but right now I can't help but think about how much better my life would be if I lived here.

7

ZOE

The sound of the shower clicking on overhead is like a release and I exhale hard, dropping my head into my hands and biting my lower lip.

I won't cry. I don't know what I'm going to do, but I know that I'm going to hold it all together the best I can. I'm going to take a deep breath, put on a happy face, and deal with this.

It could be worse. If what Ethan and Micah are saying is true, my husband didn't cheat on me. He was with someone before we met and she lied about being pregnant. This is not his fault, and I need to remember that while I handle what comes next.

It's also not Micah's fault. Out of everyone here, he's the victim. He's the one I want to protect, and I can't help but think that if I ever meet his mother—

"Mama?" Anna's sweet little voice pulls me from my thoughts. "I want ice cream."

"Ice cream, yes." I wouldn't normally give in to her like this, but I want her out of the way so Ethan and I can talk.

With Micah in the shower and Anna shoveling ice cream in her face, he and I should be able to figure some things out. "Come here, darling," I say, getting up and pulling her from her seat. "Go to the living room and I'll bring you a bowl of ice cream in a minute."

She grins and scurries away from me.

I move on autopilot as I scoop out a bowl of ice cream, adding more than I normally would so she'll be distracted for longer. Ethan enters the kitchen right as I shove a spoon into the mound of it and I hand him the bowl.

"Anna's in the living room," I tell him. "Give that to her and then you and I need to talk."

He nods, his face drawn.

While I wait for him to return, I survey the kitchen. Getting started cleaning it all up would be the smart move, but I can't seem to do anything right now. I feel like I'm broken, like a puppet with cut strings, and I lean against the kitchen counter until he returns.

"She's busy eating," he says, then points at the ceiling. "Micah's in the shower. And you're right, we need to talk." He pulls me into his arms and even though part of me wants to stand on my own two feet, I let him. There are tight knots in my back and his fingers move expertly, working them out as I exhale into his chest.

"I promise you, I never knew anything about having a son," he tells me. "I need you to believe me. I was with Rita for a very short period of time and then I never heard from her after we broke up. I never knew that she was pregnant." He lets go of me, pushing me back a bit so his eyes can search mine.

I nod. "I believe you. I'm kinda in shock right now, but I believe you."

He hugs me, pressing a kiss against my forehead. "I don't deserve you, you know that? You're too amazing."

"What do we do?" My voice is small as I whisper the question. I don't want Micah or Anna to hear our conversation and even though the shower is still running, there's a part of me afraid he might come downstairs and catch us talking about him. "We can't turn him away, right? I mean, we could call DSS and get social services involved, but he's your son, Ethan."

"I know." A long exhale. "I know. I can't imagine turning him away even though this is shocking. But really? How in the world can we let him live here? We have a good life, Zoe. I'm respected in my career, Anna is happy, you're happy. I can call DSS. Get someone else to help him. Why rock the boat?"

Why rock the boat? Is he serious? The boat was rocked years ago.

This is one of those times I know I'm going to look back on in the future and hope that I made the right decision. Even though I know, in my heart, what we need to do, I'm still scared.

"He's your son," I say, stepping back from Ethan. Even to my ears my tone is firmer than normal. "He's your son and that means we can't turn him away. There's no way I could live with that. Can you imagine? Look at the boy. He's obviously had a rough go of it. The police need to know that he showed up here in case she goes looking for him, but we can't turn him away. Who cares about anything other than helping him out?"

Ethan's silent and, for a moment, I think he's going to argue with me.

Looking past him to make sure Anna hasn't wandered

back into the kitchen, I then turn my head up to him and wait for his response.

"I don't deserve you, Zoe." He sounds pained, like even saying those words to me hurts him. "I'm serious, you're too good for me. But you don't have to do this. We don't have to do this. We can keep our life as usual. We don't have to change anything. This doesn't have to change anything. I'm serious. We have a good life and we can make sure he has one, too. But it doesn't have to be with us."

"You'd do the same for me," I tell him, even though right now I'm not so sure. Ethan is the one person I know who has dedicated his life to taking care of other people and making sure they're healthy with the best life possible, so why is he fighting this? This isn't how either of us saw our lives going, but we don't have a choice. "You'd do the same for me, right?"

"You're right, I would." This time, when he meets my eyes, there's more confidence in his gaze, and I feel my heart lift. "I'd do anything I had to for your kid, Zoe."

"And I'm going to do the same for yours. He seems like a nice kid. And as long as he needs it, he has a home here." The words are the right ones to say and I realize with a start that I mean them. I don't know anything about this kid or about what he'll be like when he's older, but I do know that I want to be there for him.

I knew from the moment I laid eyes on him that he was Ethan's. The love that I feel for my husband, for our daughter... well, maybe I'll be able to feel that someday for this boy.

Ethan exhales. Pushes his hair back from his face. I wish I could read his mind, tell what he's thinking, but I can't right now. "Thank you. I'll go up and talk to him when he gets out of the shower. Shall we put him in the guest room next to Anna's?"

I hesitate. It's one thing to open your home to someone you don't know, another entirely to possibly put your child at risk. "Put him in the guest room next to ours. That way, if he needs anything, he'll be able to call out and I can easily hear him. Tomorrow I'll call his school and explain the situation. We'll go shopping while Anna is at preschool and I'll get him everything he needs."

"When I married you I knew you were an incredible woman, but I had no idea how amazing you were." Ethan takes a deep breath and lets it out in a shudder. "Thank you, Zoe. There isn't anyone else I'd want to face this with. But if you change your mind—"

"I love you. I'm not changing my mind." The shower overhead stops and I pause. "Now, you better get up there so he knows you're there for him. I have a feeling you two have a lot to talk about, but some of it is going to have to wait until tomorrow."

He pauses. "I could try to move my surgeries for tomorrow. Take the day off so I can spend it with him. What do you think?"

That's not a bad idea. Still, even though part of me wants to include Ethan and have him handle as much of the heavy lifting as possible when it comes to Micah, I think I need to handle this part on my own. "He doesn't know where his mom is and while he'll want to connect with you, I'd like him to feel confident when he does. Comfortable. I'll get him some clothes, whatever food he loves, make him feel welcome. Maybe you can come home early, though? You two can connect then."

Ethan pauses for a moment before answering, which is

something I love about him. He never does things without thinking them through.

"I trust you," he finally says, lightly lifting my chin with one finger. "I trust you and I love you. There's nobody else I'd trust to take care of him like you will. Thank you."

That's all I need. "You're welcome," I tell him, then force a smile. "Time to go see your son. Tell him the plan for tomorrow. I'll take care of everything."

He kisses me—once, gently—then he hurries out of the kitchen to go talk to Micah. I know I need to get Anna, need to settle her before bed, but for a moment I want to be still.

Am I making the right choice?

I have no idea.

I do know that it's the only choice I can make. Micah's mom is missing. Ethan is his dad. Even though the thought of my husband with someone else makes me sick, I can't turn my back on a child.

No, Micah isn't my son. But he belongs to my husband. He needs someone to look out for him and make sure nothing bad happens to him.

I can do that. I *will* do that.

It's here, standing in my kitchen, my mind racing, that I make a promise.

I don't know where he came from, but I do know one thing. Nothing will ever hurt Micah again.

8

ZOE

Tuesday March 14

Anna won't stop staring at Micah. It wouldn't be so uncomfortable if she would say something, but all through breakfast she stared at him, her eyes wide, her mouth moving mechanically as she chewed and swallowed. I know having him here is a huge change and one she's going to have to get used to, but it's still unnerving.

Now I have both kids in the car and she's still staring at him from the back seat, her mouth hanging open a little, her hands splayed on her knees. She's in a trance, but Micah hasn't noticed. He's kept his face turned towards the window like he's been taking in the sights as we drove.

"Alright," I say, my voice a sing-song, "you're out of here, Anna Banana." After putting the car in park, I turn around and grab her foot, giving it a little wiggle before her preschool teacher comes to get her out of the car. Even though it's hard to say goodbye to her without giving her a hug, I get it.

They want to keep the line moving. They want to make sure there's no traffic jam.

They want to prevent any complete and total meltdowns. Mostly it's the kids, but I've seen some moms throw some real fits when they have to say goodbye to their babies.

"Bye-bye," she says, flapping her hand at me, then at Micah.

I watch from the corner of my eye as the boy sucks in a breath, then turns. He wiggles his fingers at her. "Bye, sis."

My breath catches in my throat. As soon as Mrs. Denise pulls Anna from the car and slams the door, I put the car back in drive and pull away from the curb.

"I like her so much," Micah says. It's the first bit of information he's willingly offered up since he appeared on our front porch yesterday. Everything else I've had to drag out of him like it hurt him to share anything personal. "I always wanted a little sister."

"Oh, yeah?" How's my voice? Is it possible he can hear how strange that sounds to me, how it rubs me wrong? It's not that we're talking about him having some nebulous girl as his little sister, we're talking about my baby.

It's strange, that's all.

"Yeah. I thought if I had someone, a little sister or brother, I wouldn't be alone all the time when my mom left."

And now my heart is breaking. Micah wanted to sit shotgun with me when we ran our errands this morning and I glance over at him. He's staring straight ahead, his jaw relaxed, but his hands are clenched tight into fists. As uncomfortable as this situation is, I have to remind myself that he's the victim here.

He's the one who hasn't had a dad in his life. And while he has had a mom around, it's not like she's been great. From the sound of it, Rita never went out of her way to be a good mother, to take care of him. To make him feel welcome.

"Well, I know Anna will love having you around to play with," I say, because what else is there to say? I can't tell him that the thought of anyone stepping into the role of a big brother for her makes me uncomfortable. Even though I can't put my finger on why that is, I know that I don't like it. But it's not his fault.

"Yeah. She seems nice." He glances at me as I pull up to a red light. "And so do you."

"Oh, Micah," I say, drumming my fingers on the steering wheel as I try to think about what to say next. Maybe I shouldn't have been so quick to tell Ethan that I had things under control with his son. That might have been a bad idea, judging by the fact that I can't think of anything to say to the boy right now.

"I'm sorry about this," he says, his voice soft as he fills the silence between us. "Showing up like that, I mean. I know it had to be a surprise. And I didn't even have anything to bring with me, so now you have to take me shopping."

There's an edge to his voice and I glance down from the road, not surprised that he's gripping his thighs as hard as possible.

"What happened isn't your fault." My heart aches for the boy and I know I need to say something to take the edge off his discomfort. "Parents are supposed to take care of their children, and you can't help the fact that your mom didn't do that. And Ethan—your dad—he didn't know that you existed. *Neither* of us did. But now we do and we're going to do everything in our power to take care of you. You don't have to worry about that. We're not turning our backs on you."

I finish my monologue as we pull up to the mall. It's not huge, not like some of the malls in larger cities, but all we need are a few shops to get him some clothes and shoes. Toiletries. Oh, and I want to pop by the grocery store to make sure I have some of his favorite foods on hand.

My head spins.

"First things first," I say, giving a nod like that's going to be enough to clear my head. "I'm going to call your school and then you and I are going to hit that mall and get you whatever you need. After that, we'll go to the grocery store and buy your favorite snacks. What are you into? Doritos? Cheetos? Oreos?"

The look he gives me is blank. "I had Doritos once at a party, but mom never kept snacks like that in the house."

Foot, meet mouth. I'm going to have to do better than constantly reminding him that his mother didn't treat him the way most kids are treated.

"Well, then we'll have to get them all," I reason, jerking my thumb at his door. "Why don't you hop out and get some fresh air while I call your school? You said you go to East Middle, right?"

"Right." He speaks over his shoulder as he opens the door and gets out, moving faster now, like he can hardly wait to be away from me. "Thank you."

"You got it. It's not a problem." I wait until he closes the door and leans against it before thumbing on my phone and looking up the number for his school. There it is. All I have to do is tap the green button and I'll reach his school and be able to explain what's going on.

But I hesitate. Then I look out the window and see that Micah's watching me. He gives a half-smile and a little wave.

I wave back, a smile on my face, but my stomach does this weird little flip thing. When he showed up at the house last night it seemed like the path was clear, like helping him was the only option Ethan and I had.

But it's one thing to think about being a good person and another entirely to do what's required of you to become one. He doesn't deserve the hand he's been dealt. It's not his fault Ethan didn't know he existed or that Rita was a terrible mom.

We would have intervened, I know it. Even though Ethan is obviously in shock about Micah existing and he wasn't sure what to do last night, I know we would have helped Micah had we known he existed. We could have sent money or supported her, gotten Rita into rehab so she could be the mother he needed, but since we never knew that she needed help, we never offered it.

Until now. I think about how sad he looked standing on our front porch last night. I think about how he watches Anna like she's the most amazing thing he's ever seen before.

How any mother could look the other way when her child needed something is beyond me, but am I doing that by inviting him into our house with Anna? Is there a possibility that, in helping him, I'm hurting her?

My head pounds with the thought.

God, I hope I'm making the right decision.

9

MICAH

Zoe was on the phone a long time. She kept looking up at me, her eyes dark even through the car window, then she'd give me a half-smile and look away.

What if she changes her mind?

I shift my feet, nerves making it difficult for me to stand still. The last thing I want is to stand here in the parking lot and wait for her to decide what she's going to do, but what other choice do I have? I have no money. I used the last of it to take a taxi to their house last night.

And I know how I look. Dirty. Unkempt. Kids have whispered those words behind me for years. I wouldn't make it very far looking the way I do. Someone would stop me. Call the cops. And then the truth of my mom would come out. And if Dad wouldn't take me in?

Foster care. I swallow hard at the thought of having to move in with someone I don't know. Someone I'm not related to.

After what seems like ages, Zoe finally gets out of the car

and slams the door. She presses her thumb against the handle and the car beeps. I didn't know you could lock cars like that.

"It's all settled, Micah," she says, and rubs her hands together like she's about to dive into a delicious meal. "I just talked to your school and told them what's going on. You're excused from classes today but they want you there tomorrow, which I said was fine. You'll be fresh and clean when I drop you off in the morning."

My tongue feels stuck to the roof of my mouth. "Great," I manage. "Thank you. So now you want to go shopping?"

She looks at me like I've lost my mind, then smiles. "Yep. Like we talked about. If you get hungry while we're out shopping, let me know. I want this to be fun."

I nod, feeling a bit silly. She had told me the plan but I wanted to double-check. My mom never managed to stick to a plan once it was made, so I guess I wanted to make sure that was going to happen with Zoe.

But the more time I spend with her, the more I see she's not at all like my mom. That's a good thing.

I hope she likes me.

I hope she lets me stay.

10

ZOE

Micah's in his room looking at all the clothes I bought him today and Anna's playing with Play-Doh at the kitchen counter when I hear the garage door rise. Exhaling hard, I wipe my hands on my apron—not that I needed one to throw a pizza in the oven—and put a smile on my face.

Today was hard.

Maybe it was ridiculous of me to think it would be a smooth transition to go from the schedule Anna, Ethan, and I have to suddenly adding a teenager to the mix, but it's been harder than I thought it would be when I came up with the plan of taking Micah shopping.

At least he asked for something specific for dinner tonight. I had to press him hard for him to tell me what he wanted, but a frozen pizza is a lot easier than making something from scratch, and I'm drained. All I want is to feed the kids, see how Ethan's day was, and take my shower.

Pass out.

Wake up and maybe tomorrow will be easier.

"Daddy!" Anna squeals as Ethan lifts her out of her high chair, spinning her in a circle, then plants a kiss on her cheek. "Daddy's home!"

"I'm home, Anna Banana," he crows, then comes to give me a kiss. I don't miss how his eyes dart around the kitchen and how he frowns a little before pulling me to him.

"He's in his room picking out something to wear for dinner," I tell Ethan. "We had a great morning and I think he wants to dress to impress."

"That's nice. And do I smell pizza?"

"Micah picked it." Anna squirms out of Ethan's grasp and books it across the kitchen. "I'll get him."

"Thanks, darling." Ethan winks at her, then turns to the fridge. "Is wine acceptable with pizza? I think I'd prefer a glass of that over a beer."

"Pretty sure it's your house and you can drink whatever you want," I say, donning some oven-safe gloves and opening the door to pull out the pizza. A wave of hot air washes over me and I breathe in the scent of the melted cheese before grabbing it and putting it, pizza stone and all, on the stove.

"Hey, where's the picture of you from our beach trip last summer?" Ethan sounds bemused and I turn to him, brushing hair back from my face as I do. "It was here," he tells me, tapping his finger on the fridge door.

"I don't know." I frown, trying to think if I saw Anna sneak it off the fridge. For a short period of time she'd been obsessed with magnets and we'd had to make the switch to using tape to hang pictures and paper on the fridge. The last thing we wanted was for her to swallow a magnet.

I'd switched back to magnets just last month. My stomach flips when I think about her possibly pulling it down and swallowing it.

"Do you think Anna took it?" I don't want to give voice to my fear but relief washes over me when Ethan answers me.

"No, the magnet is here. Only the photo is gone. Weird." He shrugs like it's no big deal and starts rummaging around in the fridge. "Wine for you?"

"Um, water, thanks." There's no way to express how long a day I had without coming across as whiny, and that's the last thing I want. The thought of drinking wine though, when I'm already feeling close to the edge, turns my stomach.

I fill glasses for Anna, Micah, and myself, and cut the pizza. Just when I'm about to go to the bottom of the stairs to call for the kids, I hear footsteps.

Take a deep breath, Zoe. Everything is fine.

"Hey," Micah says. He sounds happier than I've heard him since he showed up, and I turn in surprise. What I see surprises me.

Anna's on his hip, her skinny arms wrapped around his neck. She has her cheek pressed up against his, her eyes bright as she looks right at me. "Brudder." She laughs, then points at Micah. "My brudder."

"I taught her that." Micah beams at me, then looks at Ethan. "Oh, hi, Dad. How was work?"

Ethan doesn't immediately answer. I turn to watch as he pours a glass of wine and takes a sip before looking at Micah. "Wonderful, Micah, thanks. Did you and Zoe have fun shopping?"

"We did." He bends down, helping Anna find her footing before standing back up. "Do you like my clothes?" He holds his arms out from his body, a little awkwardly, but there's a huge smile on his face.

Ethan smiles. I'm half watching the two of them, half

watching as Anna tries to pull herself up into her highchair. Moving on autopilot, I lift her in and slide her closer to the table.

"You look great. I like the shirt." Ethan gives Micah a smile and then turns to look at me. "Thanks for taking him shopping. And am I to understand that the pizza was your idea, Micah?"

"Sure was, Dad." The boy is all smiles as he pulls out a chair and climbs into it. "It was nice of Zoe to let me choose what we were going to eat."

"Well, I wanted you to feel at home here," I say. The pizza needs to be plated and I do that quickly, pleased to have a task that I can do with my eyes closed. "I figured picking what you wanted for dinner would make you feel like you fit in here."

"You're a good mom," Micah remarks, smiling at me as he takes the plate I hand him. "Anna's so lucky. I'd love to have a mom like you."

It feels like time stops. All the air in the room has been sucked out and I look up at Ethan, my eyes searching his for help with how I should respond.

Ethan stares at me then takes a sip of wine.

"Hey, did you call the police today to let them know about Rita?" My voice is light as I sit down at the table. "You're welcome here as long as necessary, Micah, but I know your mom will be missing you."

"She won't," the boy mutters, but I ignore him, my eyes locked on Ethan.

"I thought you were calling." Ethan frowns at me. "Remember? I had a lot of patients to see today. That's why I had to cancel our father-son time this afternoon."

No, I don't remember that. What I remember is Ethan

telling me he would call the police today and come home early from work so he and Micah could have some bonding time. While I want to argue with him and prove my point, the last thing I want is to upset either of the kids. We always try to present a united front, not only in front of Anna and now Micah, but also out in the community.

It's for the best. Ethan explained it to me one time like this: Nobody in town wants to go to a doctor who can't keep his family in order. Who can't seem to get along with his wife. Although sometimes we do disagree, I know he's right. Whatever disagreement we're having isn't worth letting get out of control so people outside our marriage know something's going on.

And as for Anna and Micah? Don't they deserve stability, to be able to rest easy knowing that everything with their parents is fine? Especially since Micah is new here, since he's been through so much. I don't see a reason to make him feel uncomfortable, especially if Ethan or I can take care of the problem later.

"I must have been mistaken," I say, even though I'm pretty sure I wasn't. "Micah and I were having so much fun that I forgot."

"It's fine," Micah says.

Ethan must hear the same frustration in his voice that I do, because he gets up from the table and walks around it to Micah, shaking his head before taking the boy by the shoulders. "It's not. Zoe and I never want to make you feel unwelcome or unwanted. I don't know what's going on with your mom, but you can be here as long as you need to. You're welcome here. We're happy to have you and we'll do whatever it takes to keep you safe, to make sure you have a home you feel comfortable in."

Micah blinks, slowly, like his brain can't quite compute what he heard Ethan say, and I'm sure that's exactly what's going on. What are the chances he's ever heard any adult in his life talk to him like that?

I feel chills race through my body and I wonder if Micah feels them too. Next to him, Anna chews on a pizza crust, her grip on it so tight that nobody could peel her fingers off it. I keep my eyes locked on her for a moment to give Ethan and Micah some privacy, but when my husband sits back down, I address Micah.

"You don't need to worry about a thing. Tomorrow you'll go to school and have a great day. I'll take care of everything from here. Trust me."

"Right." He takes a deep breath. Exhales. "I trust you," he tells me, staring right into my eyes. "I know you won't let me down the way my real mom did."

His words make me shiver. It wasn't a threat, not at all, but was there malice under his words?

Is there something more to the boy than I thought I saw at first?

11

ZOE

Wednesday March 15

"Micah, we're going to be late!" I raise my voice enough to ensure he'll hear me in his room, but I don't want to yell and make him think he's in trouble. When I don't immediately hear his door open, I turn to Anna. "You stay here, got it? Let me go get Micah."

"Brudder." Anna props her hands on her hips and stares up at me. "My brudder."

"Right. Yep." It would be easy to call Micah her brother, because that's what he is, isn't he? Her half-brother, anyway. Still, even though I know I *could* say it, I can't make myself. The words are stuck in my throat, like saying them is going to make this all the more real.

Although, to be fair, how much more real can it get? He's

moved in, I've taken him shopping, I'm taking him to school as soon as he comes downstairs.

"Micah, I'm coming up!" I smile as I call out the words to take any edge off my voice. Maybe he got nervous. Maybe the pressure of going back to school while his mom is missing is too much for him. I don't know what the problem is, but I do know that if he doesn't get his butt in gear, he's going to be late.

And then Anna will be late to preschool. And I'll have to deal with snide remarks there.

"I'm coming!" Micah's door flies open right as I reach for the knob and I step back in surprise. He barrels out, his backpack high on his shoulder, brand new sneakers on his feet. "I'm so sorry. I'm coming. I'll go down right now!"

There's a note of something—fear, maybe—in his voice, and I hate that he might feel that way. Maybe Rita was mean to him, but not me. I've never been mean to a kid and I'm not starting now.

"Great," I say, still forcing a smile to my face. "Great, we can be on our way." Racing down the stairs, I grab my keys from the hook by the door and usher the two kids out to the car. Rather than climbing right in the front seat, Micah steps in front of me, blocking me from helping Anna.

"I've got her, Mom. You can hop on in to drive."

A shiver dances up my spine and, for a moment, I feel like I'm about to lose my balance. Reaching out, I grab the car, holding on for dear life like that's going to be enough to help me regain my equilibrium. Inhaling hard, I try to understand what I heard Micah say.

Maybe I misheard him? Maybe I thought I knew what he said but I missed it, or I missed the meaning, or I was having an auditory hallucination.

But no, I know that's not true. I know, as much as I wish it didn't happen, that Micah called me something he shouldn't have. He said it nonchalantly, without even looking over his shoulder at me, but it wasn't his tone of voice that made me freeze in place.

It's what he said. What he *called* me.

Mom.

"Thanks," I manage, but the word feels unfamiliar as I slide behind the wheel. My movements are all on auto-pilot as I buckle up and push the button to raise the garage door.

A moment later Micah clambers into the seat next to me and grins as he clicks his seatbelt into place. "Anna's all bucked up, so we're ready!"

"That's perfect," I manage, but the words seem to stick in my throat a little. I clear it. "Thanks for handling that for me. That definitely made the morning go smoother."

He beams. I swear, the kid beams. I was blowing a little smoke to make him feel good about what he was doing but man, it sounds like he needed some praise.

I can do this. I don't know a lot about teenagers, and I highly doubt anyone else in the world is in the same situation as we are, so I don't know who to talk to, but I can handle this. I'll help him gain some confidence, because it sounds like Rita never did that.

Micah's quiet. Shy. Almost like he's afraid to draw too much attention to himself.

"So," I say, wanting to build him up a bit more before dropping him off at school, "what are you excited about at school today?"

A quick glance. His thick bangs have fallen down over his forehead and he brushes them out of the way before answering. "I guess coming home."

"Surely you want to see friends," I say, knowing full well that I'm prying. The last thing I want is to make him uncomfortable, but I'd like to get to know more about him. "Do you have a best friend? Someone you'd like to invite over sometime?"

He perks up. I'm sure he does. What kid doesn't want to invite a friend over after school?

But a moment later he sighs. "Not really. Nobody I'm super close to." His voice is low and he picks at his jeans while he speaks.

"Well, that can always change," I say, keeping my voice as perky as possible. "You never know when someone is going to change from being just a kid you know in class to someone you're friends with. I can't wait to hear how your day goes."

We sit in silence at a red light, my blinker the only sound in the car. Even Anna is quieter than usual, and I glance in my rearview mirror to see what she's doing.

She has a piece of paper and is staring at it, but I can't tell from here what it is. Frowning, I adjust my mirror, hoping I can tell what it is.

"It's green, Mom," Micah says, his voice jerking me out of my thoughts.

"Oh, crap." I glance right and left quickly and then press down on the gas, turning left into the school. "Thanks, Micah. Hey, do you know what Anna has?"

"A photo." He mumbles the words, red creeping up his neck. Before I get a chance to ask him what's going on, I slow to a stop and he throws open the door, barreling out and slamming it behind him.

"I'll be here at three," I call, rolling down his window. "Have a good day."

He pauses, digging his toe into the sidewalk. "Bye, Mom. Thanks. And bye, Anna!"

The flow of traffic guides us on and I pull away from the front of the school. Still, right before we turn out onto the main road, I glance back at him. He's still standing right where I left him, his eyes locked on the back of the car.

"Weird," I mutter, then hope Anna didn't hear me. "Hey, kiddo, what do you have?"

"A picture." She holds it up above her head, but I can only see the back of it. "From my brudder."

"It's from Micah?" I ask, and she nods. "He gave it to you?"

"Yep." She pops the "p", something she recently learned how to do. "It's mine."

"I can't wait to see it," I say, glancing back at her after passing someone who was inching along.

Her face darkens.

"I'll give it back, of course," I say, grinning at her. "I only want to see it because I bet it's fabulous."

She watches me, her face solemn, her eyes wide.

"Weird," I mutter to myself again, then I twist the radio knob, Dolly Parton's voice chasing my worries away. Sure, I have a lot to do today, and I don't love the way Micah is inserting himself into our family and calling me *Mom*, but what am I supposed to do about that?

There's no good way to stop it without crushing him, and the poor kid has been through enough already.

"Alright, kiddo," I say as I pull up to Anna's preschool. Already Mrs. Denise is headed towards the car to get her out. "You have a wonderful day. I'll be here in a few hours to pick you up, then we'll have the afternoon together before we go get Micah."

She's still holding that photo Micah gave her. I'm dying to see what it is. Probably nothing, knowing kids and how they can make big deals out of anything, no matter how small and unimportant the thing actually is, but there's something about this that makes me uncomfortable.

Like Micah knows something I don't.

"Hi, Mrs. Denise," I say, pushing down my panic and sounding as cheery as possible. "Anna grabbed that photo before she left the house, but I need it back. Can you get it from her and hand it to me?"

Anna hears what I'm saying and her eyes dart back and forth between us like she's going to be able to stop me from getting what I want. I know she'll probably throw a fit when Mrs. Denise takes the paper from her, but right now I don't care.

I can't get rid of the feeling that I need to see what it is.

Mrs. Denise grabs it and yanks it free from Anna's fist. "Thank you, Anna," she coos. "Your mama needs that and you and I need to go play. We're making macaroni necklaces today."

"Anna, that sounds so fun," I say, but my eyes are locked on the photo. "Thank you, Mrs. Denise."

"No problem at all." She has Anna on her hip and she leans forward to hand me the photo. "That's... interesting, Zoe. Quite the art project."

I force a smile that feels like it's mostly teeth and take the photo from her, my hands shaking as I turn it around to look at it.

It's me.

Or, part of me.

12

ZOE

My hand shakes as I stare at the photo. Behind me, someone honks the horn but I can't tear my eyes away from my face.

It's my face. Vaguely, I remember Ethan mentioning the photo was missing from the fridge, but I didn't know then where it had gone, and I hadn't had the energy to look into it.

I know, now.

It's—

"Mrs. Steele?" The director of Anna's preschool, Lauren Trainer, raps her knuckles on my window. "I need you to move your car if you can. Is there a problem?"

"No problem," I lie, dropping the photo into my lap and slamming my foot down on the gas. I'm still in park from Anna getting out and my engine roars. Heat flames my face as I put the car in drive and press down on the gas again. This time, I pull away from the curb, my heart beating in my throat, my hands slick with sweat.

I pull out from the school and into the gas station next door, then park my car. Turn off the engine. Grab the photo.

Frankenphoto.

It's me. My face, anyway. My head is tilted at a jaunty angle like I'm excited about what's going on. I'm grinning from ear to ear, but that's the only thing I recognize from the photo. My head is on a body I don't recognize, the sizing off so my head is too big for the body. And I'm holding someone's hand.

I look closer.

Micah.

I'm holding Micah's hand.

My stomach twists and I drop the photo again, grabbing the door handle and throwing it open so I can lean out into the fresh air. I gulp in the sweet morning air, tainted as it is with gas fumes, and finally catch my breath.

"What the hell is this?" I mutter, sitting up and slamming my door. Some man pumping gas in a bright red Jeep stares at me from across the parking lot, but I don't care about him. I don't care about anything but trying to wrap my mind around what Anna was holding.

She didn't do this, I'm sure of it. She doesn't have access to scissors or glue, but Micah does. He's tall enough to get into the craft cupboard and help himself to whatever he wants.

And it looks like he did.

Using my fingernail, I try to pick up the edge of my head so I can see what's underneath, but he did a great job gluing me down. I'm stuck, but even without seeing whose face I'm covering, I think I know.

Micah looks so young in this photo. So happy. He's clinging to the person's hand like they're the only one in the world who's on his side.

It has to be Rita.

"Why would you do that, Micah?" I ask, tracing my finger over my face. It makes no sense why he'd cut my face out of a photo and plaster me over his mom's. Why would he think that was okay, that it was a good idea, that I wouldn't freak out?

Maybe he didn't think I'd find out. But then why would he give the photo to Anna? He had to know, on some level, that she wouldn't be able to keep something like this to herself, that I'd find it eventually.

Which means that he wanted me to find it.

That thought is even more disturbing than the idea that he might have made this little craft project and hidden it from me. Sure, it would have been beyond creepy to discover it on my own when I went into his room for something, but having it basically handed to me through my daughter?

My skin crawls. I always thought that was a load of crap, that there was no way anyone's skin could ever feel like that, but now I know it's true. It feels like there are a million ants marching up and down my arms, and even though the sun is warm through the windshield, I have goosebumps.

"I need to call Ethan," I manage, gasping out the words. My head hurts and I can't wrap my mind around what's going on, but Ethan will have some insight. My hands tremble as I pull my phone from my purse and dial his number.

My face stares at me from the passenger seat and I reach out, flipping the photo over so I don't have to look at myself.

Someone picks up on the second ring.

"Ethan, hey, I need to talk to you." The words burst out of me. I feel completely unable to hold them back, to do anything other than panic right now.

"Mrs. Steele, hi. This is Bonnie! Dr. Steele left his phone

at the nurse's station in case he had any calls while he was in surgery. Can I help you with something?"

Bonnie. Oh, I know Bonnie, with her little button nose and her blonde curls. I know the way she watches people and whispers about them, how she trades information as currency, and how she'd probably love nothing more than to tell everyone at the hospital what's going on at our house.

If Ethan hasn't mentioned Micah—and I doubt he has, not without figuring out a way to keep from hurting his reputation in this small town—then I'm not going to be the one to drop that bombshell right in the lap of the hospital's biggest gossip.

"Oh, Bonnie, hi," I say, trying to sound more relaxed than I feel right now. "Thank you, but I can wait until Ethan has time to call me back."

"Are you sure? You sounded pretty frantic. I can take him a message, you know."

"No, no." I take a deep breath. "That won't be necessary, but thank you. I'll talk to him later."

She pops her gum. Are nurses supposed to be chewing gum when they're at work? I close my eyes and force myself to take some deep breaths so I don't scream.

That would certainly give her something to run her mouth about. News of me screaming at her would make it all the way around the hospital before Ethan got out of surgery.

"Well, if you change your mind, you know how to find me. All you have to do is call your husband." She laughs.

I don't.

Maddening. She's maddening.

"I hope you have the day you deserve, Bonnie," I say, and hang up before she can try to rub her two brain cells together and figure out what I meant by that. If she wraps her mind around what I said, then I have no doubt I'll hear about it from Ethan when he gets home, but that's not something I'm going to worry about right now.

I'm going to worry about Micah.

And why he cut my head out of a photo and glued it to his mother's body.

I'm going to call the police and tell them Rita is missing. That we're looking after him. That things are *fine*, thank you, but they need to find her.

Alive, hopefully.

13

MICAH

It was stupid of me to think that new shoes would be enough to make the cool kids not hate me any longer. Even my Nikes, which I'm pretty sure I saw half the basketball team wearing last week, weren't enough to stop the taunts.

The comments.

The sideways glances.

But I did my best to ignore them. It felt amazing to run in gym class without my toes jamming into the ends of my shoes. And I have to admit that I liked the way I saw two girls looking at me during lunch. I took a long, hot shower last night and used the body wash and shampoo Zoe gave me, so I was all clean and ready for a good day.

But it wasn't all good, not really. Lunch was nice, because I had food Zoe packed, and those two girls were cute. But the rest of the day... not great. I know not to tell Zoe that, though. My mom never wanted to hear when things were bad at school. She only wanted to hear the version of my day where things went the way I wanted them to and where I was happy.

But I wasn't happy, not really. Not at school. Not then. It could have been worse, it could have been better.

That's something my mom used to say when she'd return from being missing for days at a time, and thinking about her makes my heart hurt. Pushing that thought of her from my mind, I hitch my backpack higher on my shoulder and look at the line of cars driving up to the school for pickup.

Zoe promised me she'd be here and I believe her. She hasn't done anything so far that would make me think she'd forget me, but what if she did? What if she and Anna got so busy that she forgot me?

Or what if they found Mom?

Now I feel like I could throw up. The endless line of cars coming up to the school for pickup is maddening, especially when I don't see my car.

I called Zoe "Mom." Did that upset her? Did I push it too fast? She takes care of me in a way I've never been taken care of before and I like it. I think she honestly likes me, that she enjoys spending time with me.

Maybe I shouldn't have called her that. Maybe this is her way of punishing me for doing that. Or maybe I wasn't nice enough with Anna. I love having a little sister I can play with and talk to, but maybe Zoe doesn't like that I'm not spending enough time with her.

I'm so confused.

My legs feel weak and I sink down to the ground, pressing my hands over my ears so I can try to block out some of the chatter from the kids around me. Everyone else is excited about going home and spending the afternoon with their families. Some kids are talking about what they're going to have for dinner but all I can think about is whether or not Zoe is going to show up.

"Micah?" There's a hand on my shoulder and I force myself to look up. Mrs. Myers, my homeroom teacher, stares down at me. She has honey-colored hair and braces.

I like her. Before her, I didn't know adults could have braces.

"How are you?"

I shrug. "I'm fine. I don't know if my mom—if Zoe—is going to come get me."

"Why wouldn't she get you?" She's crouched next to me now, the look of concern on her face so obvious it almost hurts to look at her. "Did something happen?"

I don't answer. I can't tell Mrs. Myers about calling Zoe "Mom" or the photo I gave Anna. It was stupid to take Zoe's photo from the fridge and cut off her head but I wanted to see what she would look like as my mother.

"Well, why don't I wait with you? What color car does she drive?"

"Um, blue." I drop my hands down to my sides and look at the cars. From my vantage point on the ground I can't see much of anything, so I force myself to stand up. "Blue, with four doors. So my little sister can sit in the back."

As soon as the words are out of my mouth, I wince. Will she think I'm weird for saying that? Will all of the teachers laugh about me behind my back when they go in to clean their classrooms?

But she doesn't laugh. She points. "Like that one, right there?"

My head whips around and I use one hand to shield my eyes from the sun. Yes, that's it. I'm sure that's it. It's a shiny blue, not the boring blue that a lot of people have for their cars, but bright and shiny, and clean, like Zoe washes it every single day because she's so proud of it.

"That's it," I say, and I'm unable to keep the excitement out of my voice. "That's her."

"Great." Mrs. Myers pats me on the shoulder. "I'll see you tomorrow in homeroom, right? Make sure you ask for help if you need it with your math homework."

"I will," I say, but I'm barely paying attention to her. My feet feel like they're moving on autopilot as I walk towards the blue car. I see Zoe behind the wheel, her eyes flicking from side to side until she sees me.

And then she smiles.

It doesn't quite reach her eyes but it's still a smile, so I'll take it.

Bolstered by that, I run to the car and throw open the passenger door. From the backseat I hear Anna.

"Brudder!"

"Hi, Anna." I feel like I'm going to burst with pride as I get in the car. I know other kids are watching me, wondering who's picking me up from school, wondering why I'm not walking home or taking the bus, and I love it. I want everyone to know that things are looking up for me. That things are changing. That I'm going to start having the good days I pretend to have.

And it's all because my mom is gone.

14

ZOE

The smile on my face feels as fake as can be, but I still keep it plastered on there, turning my head so I can watch as Micah gets in the car. I hear him greet Anna, see the way she excitedly throws her hands into the air at the sight of him.

Even though I feel terrible about not being excited about having this boy in my car right now, he and I have a few things to talk about.

The photo, mostly.

"How was your day?" Now my eyes are trained on the road as I pull away from the school. The principal watches the line of cars, her arms crossed, like she's fully expecting a parent to pull a Fast and Furious and zip out of the parking lot, yanking the emergency brake to drift into traffic, narrowly missing the kids who live close enough to the school to walk home.

"It was good." The words explode out of Micah. "I think I did pretty well in class and I paid attention and I might make some friends at lunch."

His words sound happy but there's still a lot of pain under them and I turn to look at him. "You might make some friends at lunch?"

"Maybe." His voice is quiet.

"Are you telling me you honestly don't already have friends? There's nobody you sit with or anything?"

Now he shakes his head, the movement slow, almost like it hurts. "Nooo," he says, drawing out the word. "I don't have friends. Nobody wants to be friends with someone whose mom is a druggie and always disappears."

Ouch. Here I am, ready to confront him over his creepy little art project, and the kid is obviously in pain. I clear my throat, adjust my grip on the steering wheel. "Well, they're missing out. I'm glad you may have found some people to spend time with."

"Me too." He nods enthusiastically. "It's exciting, right? And maybe, one day, when I have friends, I can have them over to the house. What do you think?"

I swallow hard. "I think having friends over sounds amazing," I say. Each of my words is careful, measured. I want to believe the best in this kid, I do, but he and I have some things to talk about. "What do you think you'd like to do with them?"

He starts talking, really getting into his ideas of what to do with his friends, but I'm barely listening. Even though I've driven this road home so many times I'm pretty sure I could do it in my sleep, I keep my eyes locked on the road. My hands are at ten and two. I use my blinker every time I turn and make sure I leave enough space between me and the car in front of me.

By the time we pull into the garage, Micah is finally slowing down talking about having friends over.

"I'm so excited to have a mom who won't care if I want to have friends come by," he says, turning to me with a small smile on his face. He looks happier than I've seen him in a while, but then I notice the smile doesn't quite reach his eyes.

I should ask him what's wrong, but I'm not going to. There's an uncomfortable feeling in the pit of my stomach and I don't want to hear about his day. I'm going to ignore the half-smile he has and pretend he's really that happy. Pushing him for the truth would be the right thing to do, but I can't forget the way he made me feel earlier. How violated. How creeped out.

"Let's get Anna inside and I'll make an afternoon snack," I say. My cheeks hurt from holding a fake smile, but he doesn't seem to notice.

"I got her!" He moves fast, throwing open the car door and hopping out to help Anna out of her seat.

I sit for a moment in the car, listening to it click as the engine cools, then finally follow the two of them into the house.

"Let's go play in my room while Mom makes a snack," Micah tells Anna, but I stop him.

"Hey, I need to talk to you," I say, still smiling. Is this what it would feel like to be a mannequin? Like my face is made of plastic and showing any real emotion would make my skin crack and flake off? "Anna, you go upstairs and pull out a toy to play with Micah. He'll be with you in a minute."

"Okay!" She scurries out of the kitchen towards the stairs.

Micah turns slowly towards me, the smile on his face fading when he's finally facing me. "Did I do something wrong?" His voice is small, smaller than I've heard since he showed up on our front porch. Yesterday? Two days ago? Time is meaningless right now and I can't seem to focus on when things are happening.

"No, but I wanted to talk about the photo you gave Anna." It's on the counter between us and I pick it up to hand it to him, grateful my hand doesn't tremble as I do. "Will you please tell me about it?"

He stares at it. Looks up at me. For a moment, I don't think he's going to reach out and take it from me, but he finally does, gripping it by the corner like he's afraid he'll ruin it otherwise. While he takes it, I stare at his face, looking for any emotion.

Is he upset I'm asking him about it? Surprised? I can't tell. If he's wearing a mask, his is as professional as mine.

"I made this," he tells me.

"I figured." My voice is light, right? Chipper and easy-going?

"I hope you don't hate it," he says. "I just... my mom isn't ever there for me and you are and you've made me feel so welcome. I wanted to know what it would look like if you'd been my mom this entire time, what it would be like to see pictures of the two of us." He stares up at me, blinking hard like he's going to cry. "I thought it would be nice to see how my life could have been."

My legs feel weak. I reach out for the counter and brace myself on it as I stare at Micah. His face is turned up towards mine, his eyes wide, glistening with tears.

"Micah," I say, and my voice is a whisper, "was it really that bad with your mom?"

He lets out a sob. The photo drops from his hand and flutters to the floor, but neither of us look at it. At the same time, he steps forward, his arms out, and I do the only thing I know to do, the only thing any woman in my position would do, because there is no other option, is there?

I ignore the photo on the floor. I ignore that it's flipped over and my smiling face is staring at me from Rita's body, and I hug Micah, pulling him in to my chest and squeezing him tight as he sobs.

He cries like that, held against me, his arms tight around my waist, tight like he's afraid I'm going to let go of him and float away, and when he finally takes a deep, shuddering breath and takes a step back, I don't even blink at what he says next.

15

ZOE

"I always wanted a mom like you. I hope that's okay." Micah stares at me with watery eyes.

I blink at him, unable to come up with anything to say in response. I could tell him that it's fine, that I understand, but I don't, do I? No, I never had a mother who left me at home by myself so she could go off looking for drugs. I never had to worry about whether or not there was going to be food in the kitchen or if we'd even had power.

Growing up comfortably middle-class, none of that was ever a worry for me. Sure, my clothes might not have always been name brand, and we definitely didn't take a vacation every summer when the rich kids at school did, but I didn't want for anything.

Not really.

So I can't tell him I understand, not without lying through my teeth, and I don't want to do that to this boy when it's obvious he's struggling so much to even look me in the eyes and tell me the truth. So, instead, I do the only thing I know that will help calm him down.

At least, I hope it will.

"You're safe here, Micah," I tell him, because that should allow him to relax some and will also hopefully remind him that this isn't permanent.

It isn't, right?

I still have to call the police. I got so distracted with the doctored photo he gave Anna and then it was time to pick her up from preschool and get him from school. Maybe I'm dragging my feet on doing it because I'm partly afraid of what they're going to say to me.

I want to do what's right by him. By Ethan.

But I can't keep ignoring the fact that he might be dangerous. That his mom might have messed him up.

And that I invited him into my house without knowing if he's safe.

"You go upstairs and see what Anna's doing," I say, that same forced smile back on my face. "I have a phone call to make and then I'll bring a snack upstairs. How does that sound?"

"Sounds good." He sniffs hard, wipes his nose with his shirt, then gives me a small smile. "Do you mind if I call you Mom? I don't want to upset you but you feel like my mom." He pauses, then speaks faster, like he's trying to fix what he said, "I mean you feel like how a mom should be."

I swallow hard. "You can call me whatever will make you feel better."

"Thanks, Mom." Even though his eyes are still brimming with tears, he manages a smile. "I'll go see my little sister."

"Great," I say, but my voice is quiet, even to my ears, and I don't know that he hears it as he spins away from me and runs for the stairs. His feet pound on them as he tears up to the second floor and I hear him call for Anna as he reaches the top.

For a moment, I stand still, taking it all in, trying to figure out what to do next.

Then it hits me. My phone. I have to call the police.

911? No, this isn't an emergency, not like that. I don't need an officer speeding to the house with lights and sirens to try to... what? Save me from a teenager?

No, it's not an emergency. Not yet.

Oh, God.

With a few taps on the screen I find and dial the non-emergency number for the local police.

The woman who answers sounds wide-awake and on top of it. "Greenbriar police. This is Greta. How can I help you?"

"Greta, hi. My name is Zoe Steele and I'm calling to report someone missing."

"What's their name?" There's tapping on a keyboard then a pause while she waits for my response.

"Rita..." Ethan told me, but it takes me a minute to remember it. "Miller. Her last name is Miller."

"And when was she last seen?"

Good question. Without knowing for sure, I'm not sure what to say to her so instead I launch into an explanation of what's going on. "She's the mother of my husband's son," I say, desperate to explain myself. "He showed up at our house a couple of days ago and said his mother went missing, that she does this from time to time but she hadn't come back yet. So he came here to see if we could help him."

A pause. "Did they have a custody agreement?"

I shake my head, then remember she can't see me. "No, we didn't know he existed until he showed up. It was all very sudden. He wasn't here, then he was. I haven't ever met the woman."

Silence. Then, tapping. When she speaks again I can hear the myriad of questions swirling under the words she does speak. "Do you have her address?"

"No, I don't. But the school would, right? I changed it to our address so they would know where to reach us, but maybe they would still have it on record? I bet I could call and get it for you."

"Do you know where his mother works?"

"No. I... I can ask Micah. Do you want me to have him come downstairs so I can talk to him now?"

"Mrs. Steele," Greta says, with a sigh. "If Micah's mother—"

"Rita," I interject.

"Right, Rita. She's an adult, and without any information on where we can find her or how to reach her, I'm sorry, but I don't know how much help I can be. We can put out a BOLO so officers are looking for her when they're on patrol, but if she doesn't want to be found, she won't be."

"I worry that something bad may have happened to her."

Her tone changes. "Do you have any reason to believe something did? Did Micah say something to you to indicate she might be hurt or in danger?"

"Not exactly," I say, backpedaling. "But he indicated that she doesn't usually disappear for this long. That he thinks something might have happened to her, but that he doesn't know for sure."

"Mrs. Steele, is Micah safe at your house with his father?"

What kind of a question is that? "Of course he is."

"Then I'll have officers look for Rita. We'll keep an eye

out for her and hopefully we'll find her. Get me her address and I can send officers by there."

"Great, I'll do that." I look at the clock and frown. "Micah should know his address, but if he doesn't remember it, I'll ask the school tomorrow and get back to you."

I can't imagine him not knowing his old address, but what do I know about the kid?

"That's fine." Now that we're wrapping up the conversation, Greta sounds more in control. "You said Micah's there with you?"

Okay, so the conversation isn't wrapping up.

"He is. He's upstairs right now."

"Great. What's your address?"

I rattle it off to her. "Is something wrong?"

"Not at all." She's typing, her fingers flying across the keyboard. "But I am going to send an officer out to talk to him. If his mother has been missing that long and he's been alone, we need to speak with him. Make sure he's not in crisis. Make sure there isn't anything he could tell us that would help us find her. Is now a good time for an officer to come by?"

I glance at the clock, but what am I going to say? No? "Now's fine."

"Perfect, Mrs. Steele. Do you need help with anything else right now?"

Yes. "No." *I need help because I don't know how to handle a teenage boy.* "Everything will be fine. We'll take care of Micah until we find his mom."

"Thank you, Mrs. Steele. It's always easier for the child when they can stay with family and we don't have to get social services involved. Foster care is a wonderful option for kids who don't have any other choice but can be very traumatizing for some children. You call back when you have his old address or give it to the officer when he gets there."

"I will, thank you. You have a good afternoon." I hang up and stare at the phone in my hand before turning to put it on the counter.

Micah's standing in the doorway, silent, staring at me.

"Holy crap, Micah," I say, dropping my phone with a thud to the counter and putting my hand on my heart. It's pounding. "You scared me. Is everything okay?"

"Yeah. How are you?"

"I'm fine," I say, ignoring the fact that I don't like him eavesdropping. How did he even get downstairs without me hearing him? I thought the second step up from the first floor always squeaked, but he must have figured it out and skipped it. "I was talking to the police about your mom. They're going to look for her, but we need your address. Can you give it to me?"

He pauses, chewing on his lower lip. Is that a tell? Is he lying to me? I stare at him, trying to read his mind and wishing more than anything that I could tell what he's thinking.

"Sure," he finally says. "212 Brookdale Avenue."

"212 Brookdale," I mutter, grabbing a piece of paper from by my planner and scribbling it down. "Great, Micah, that's great. An officer wants to come by and I'll give it to them. That way, they can head out to your house and check for your mom."

"A cop is coming here?" He taps his fingers against his thigh.

"Yep. They want to check on you." I pause, waiting for a response. When I don't receive one, I continue, "Now, how about that snack?"

"Thanks, yeah." He scuffs his toe into the floor and then glances up at me. "Anna's playing in her room and I'm going to go join her.

"Sounds great." I already have my back to him so I can dig through the cupboards and find something for the two of them to eat. Chips and salsa are too messy for them to have upstairs. I don't want to give them cookies, not when dinner is a few hours away.

There. In the back, on the second shelf, a box of granola bars. I have to get way up on my tiptoes to grab them, but I do, my fingers brushing the box before I snag it, then I turn around, triumphant.

"Granola bars it is," I say, but my voice fades.

He's gone.

And I never heard him leave.

16

MICAH

"Micah, I need you to come in here." It's Mom, her voice kind and gentle, like she's talking to an animal that might easily spook, and even though I hate the fact that my first instinct is to run for the door and leave the house, leave this all behind, I stand up and walk into the living room.

There's an officer on the leather sofa, his back to me. I stare at the back of his head for a moment, taking in his funny haircut, how stiff and straight his back is. Mom's sitting across from him and she gives me a small smile, then gestures for me to sit in the chair next to her.

"Officer Barnwell, this is Micah. Micah, Officer Barnwell came by from the police department to talk to you about your mom and see if you can remember anything that might help them find her."

Oh, no. Before, when I was younger, if you had asked me if I ever wanted anything bad to happen to my mom, I would have probably cried. I would have told you *no*, that I loved her, that she was everything to me, but now I know better.

I know how willing she is to walk away from me and let me fend for myself. I know how willing she is to put her needs ahead of mine. And now that I have a mom who loves me and who isn't afraid to put me first, I don't want to lose that.

I'll say anything to keep from losing that.

"Hi, Micah." The officer smiles at me as I sit down in the chair next to Mom. The fabric is soft and the cushion gives way as I sink into it. "Thanks so much for coming in here to talk to me."

I swallow hard before I'm able to find my voice. "You're welcome."

"Mrs. Steele here tells me that your mom goes missing from time to time; is that true?"

I glance at Mom. Her hands are resting on her knee and she's smiling at me. I'm a bundle of nerves right now but she looks completely unbothered.

"She does." I nod. Clear my throat. "She goes missing and then comes back, telling me it won't happen again. She's off doing drugs while she's gone," I offer. "I take care of myself."

The officer's mouth is tight. "It sounds like you were one of the last people to see her before she left this time. Did she give you any information that might let you know where she was going?"

Mom stiffens. I see it out of the corner of my eye, how she sits up a little bit straighter and looks at me a bit harder, like she can't wait to hear what I'm going to say.

"I don't think so." I'm trying to think, I honestly am. I didn't want her to leave this last time, even though she promised me it was different than the other times. I remember getting so, so angry with her. I was angry with her for leaving me, for making me feel bad.

I wanted to beg her to stay but I knew that wasn't going to work. So instead I got mad. And she got mad at me for getting angry, for not trusting her. She tried to tell me something about how she was going to change our lives for the better, but I didn't believe her.

She dressed up, nicer than I've seen her dress up before. And then I got angrier and angrier.

But I don't tell the officer that. I don't want Mom to hear me talk about how angry I can get.

"She looked nice," I offer, wanting to give the two of them something. They want to find her, I know they do. Mom looks like she might cry and I reach out to take her hand. "She looked nice and told me to stay in the house, that she'd be back."

"But she didn't indicate how long she'd be gone?" The officer has a little pad of paper out and scratches a few words on it before looking up at me.

"She never told me," I say, then think better of it. "No, that's not entirely true. She would tell me sometimes that she would only be gone a day or so, but that wasn't always true. Sometimes she'd say she'd be back in a day but wouldn't be back for a week." I shrug.

Mom squeezes my hand.

Officer Barnwell's eyes flick down to where we're holding hands, but he doesn't say anything. I dare him to. She's my mom.

"We're almost done, Micah. I know this is hard, but I have one more thing I want to ask you. Do you know any of your mom's friends? Did you ever meet any of them and remember their names? That might make it a little easier for us to find her."

"I never met her friends," I say, shaking my head. It's not a lie, not exactly. There was often a revolving door of people coming in and out of the house, but that doesn't mean I know them. It means they were there, then they weren't, and sometimes my mom stayed behind when they left.

But most of the time she didn't.

Besides, nobody came around the house before she left. I feel confident that they don't know where she is.

"Well, that's that then." Officer Barnwell glances down at the notepad in his hand then flicks his wrist, snapping it shut. He slips it into a pocket on his shirt and then tucks his pen in next to it. "If you think of anything you want to tell me, Micah, tell Mrs. Steele. I'll leave my card with her."

"I will." For some reason, I don't think correcting him and telling him that Zoe is "Mom" is a good idea.

"Thank you, Micah." Mom turns to me. "Why don't you go upstairs and get Anna and you two wash up for dinner? We can have a picnic on the back porch if you'd like."

"Sounds great." I stand, then give the officer a nod before leaving the room. A picnic on the porch sounds wonderful, even if I did have to talk to this officer to get it. I'll think of it as my little reward for doing a good job. I was honest with him, but not too honest.

Too honest might make everything fall apart.

Right as I'm about to head up the stairs, I hear Mom's voice and I slow down, wanting to know what she might say to the officer when I'm not around.

"Of course he's welcome to stay here, Officer Barnwell. But it's strange, isn't it? I have a weird feeling about all of this, like something isn't right."

He murmurs something, but his voice is too low for me to catch what he's saying.

"No, I guess you never know." Mom's agreeing with him. "I trust it will all work out, though."

My cheeks burn. *Of course* it's all going to work out.

I finally have the family I deserve. The one I've read about in books. The one other kids at school have, with parents who care and a nice house and a little sister.

There's no going back from this.

17

ZOE

"I'm telling you," I say to Ethan, pointing my toothbrush at him to get my point across, "he's super quiet. Kinda sneaks around."

Ethan frowns. He leans back against the bathroom counter, his strong arms crossed on his bare chest. We're almost ready for bed and I, for one, am so tired I feel like I could fall asleep standing up talking to him. He has to be tired too, what with his busy day at work.

But even though I'm exhausted, I still haven't told him everything about the day.

"Does he sneak around or is he so used to staying out of his mom's way that he's afraid to draw any unwanted attention?" Ethan raises his eyebrows and grabs the water cup from between our twin sinks. "We don't know what it was like for him living with Rita."

Now I feel bad.

"You're right." I heave a sigh and grab the cup from Ethan to rinse. "It's funny, because I know that things haven't been good for him but it's still a disruption to our life. He deserves better, though, and I'm going to give it to him."

For a moment I debate telling him about the photo I found that he'd Frankensteined together with my head and Rita's body. I could tell him about Micah saying he didn't have any friends at school. There are a lot of things I could tell him, but I know how busy Ethan is and how much stress he's under every single day at work. Putting more pressure on him by telling him what's been going on with Micah isn't going to help matters.

"I'm glad that he has us," I say, nodding as I speak. "What would he do if he hadn't found us? If his mom hadn't told him about you before she left this last time? Who knows where he'd be."

"Who knows." Ethan pauses before continuing. "You know, Zoe, if this is too much—"

"That's not a discussion we're having," I tell him, reaching out and putting my hand on his arm. "He needed a home and we opened ours to him. I know you're worried about how people will see this, with you having a child before we got married, but they're going to have to get over it. Micah needs a home. He's staying."

Ethan exhales hard. "You're right. Of course you're right. We can't kick him out."

"Right." I lean up and kiss him, smiling against his lips when I feel his arm slip around my waist. "He deserves the love he's never gotten before and we're going to be the ones to give it to him. Trust me, Ethan, I've got this."

"And as for everyone in town talking?"

There it is. That concern he has from time to time that things will fall apart, that people will start talking bad about him, about our family. I know how important it is for his reputation to stay spotless, but nobody can look at a child and say that they're a mistake.

It's not fair to the kid.

"They'll talk," I say, "and so you need to get ahead of it. Oh, I know. Mention it to Bonnie." I grin and then laugh at my idea, throwing my head back. "Seriously, Ethan, she would be the person to tell. You didn't know you had a child and now we're stepping up to give this boy the home he deserves. She'll eat it up. Nobody will hold it against you."

A heavy sigh and he runs his hand through his hair, pushing it back from his forehead. "I want to believe you're right, Zoe, but you know how people are. They put surgeons up on pedestals. Think we're God."

I don't mention that part of the reason some people might think surgeons are God is because of the way surgeons tend to act.

"But you're not," I say, stepping in between him and the counter so he'll look at me. "You're not perfect, but now you get the opportunity to be the perfect father. Trust me, Ethan, this is a good thing."

He doesn't respond. Time to change tactics. Micah might have creeped me out today but I'm not going to turn my back on him. There's no way I'm going to let Ethan turn his back on Micah and the family he deserves.

Besides, the police don't think Micah's done anything wrong. They're trained to tell when someone is lying or trying to hide something. If they think he's an innocent kid suffering because of his mom's choices, then that's got to be all it is.

I mean, come on. Who in the world could be raised by someone like Rita and not be a little messed up?

"Micah told me his old address and gave it to the police

to pass it on. They're going to check for Rita to make sure there wasn't any sign of foul play."

Ethan's eyes snap from his reflection in the mirror to me. "Do you think that's necessary?"

I shrug. "Yeah, I mean, what else is there to do? Can you imagine if Rita shows up and tries to take Micah back? Would you be willing to fight for him? And what if she's dead? He deserves to know, don't you think?"

He doesn't answer my questions. "You're all-in, aren't you?"

"With Micah?" I pause, thinking—about how he sat on the chair, his head down, his voice quiet as he talked to the police—then nod. "Yeah, I am. He deserves more than he's had. He has a kind heart, Ethan, like you do. He's like you." I rest my hand on his chest. "I want to give him the home every child should have."

"You are the most incredible woman, Zoe," he tells me, cupping the back of my neck and looking right into my eyes. I love it when we stand like this, like he can see into my soul and he loves what he sees there. Never did I think I'd meet anyone who loved me the way Ethan does.

"You make it easy," I tell him, then shrug. "This is the right thing to do, Ethan. I believe it. We'll make sure Micah has a home, make sure he has love. If Rita shows back up, we'll deal with it then."

"I doubt she will." Ethan takes my hand and leads me from the bathroom, flicking off the light as we go. "Rita was always flighty, and if Micah is telling the truth about how long she's been gone, she might have finally left for good. I wouldn't worry too much about it."

He's probably right, but even as we climb into bed and turn off our lamps, I can't slow my mind from racing a million miles a minute. Now that Ethan and I have had the discussion and I know Micah is staying with us, I want to make sure nobody ever takes him.

He deserves more than what Rita gave him. If I'm being honest, even thinking about his biological mom and how she treated him infuriates me.

No, if Micah is going to stay here for any period of time, then he's going to stay for as long as possible. I know the police are following up tomorrow at his house to make sure they don't think anything bad happened to Rita, but I think I will, too.

Just in case.

Not that I'll find anything they miss, but why not swing by? It'll put my mind at ease, if nothing else.

It's a house. Sure, I know Micah said growing up there was pretty terrible, but it's a house.

What's the worst that could happen?

18

MICAH

Thursday March 16

The mountain of pancakes in front of me is so daunting I don't think I could ever eat my way through it but I'm determined to try. Across from me Anna is already digging in, syrup smeared across her cheeks, one hand holding a fork in a death-grip, the other hanging tight to a stuffed dog.

"Do you want me to cut your pancakes into bites?" Mom leans over me, her long hair falling down in front of me.

I lean forward and breathe her in. Her shampoo is floral and delicious. Not at all like what my house smelled like before I came to live here.

"I can do it," I say, grabbing the knife next to my plate and carving into the stack. The pancakes are light and fluffy and swimming in syrup and I stuff a bite in my mouth as I watch Mom.

She's packing my lunch. I don't think I've ever taken a packed lunch before. My old mom always said that was one of the benefits of being poor, that I'd get free breakfast and lunch at school, but it never felt like a perk.

It felt like a bullseye on my back.

"Hey, Micah, do you want an apple or a fruit cup in your lunch?" Mom turns around, holding up both of my options. "They both look pretty good."

"Apple." I take another bite of pancakes. "Thanks."

"You got it." She busies herself at the counter and I dig into my pancakes.

The radio plays some sad country song about a man's wife leaving him and his dog getting run over, but even that doesn't ruin my mood. Everything here is so perfect, it's hard for me to think that anything in my life could ever be bad again.

Mom zips up my lunchbox—a new one we bought together—and brings it over to me. "Let me put this in your backpack. We're gonna run out of time before we have to get in the car, so I'll help you along a bit."

"Great, thanks." Even though I trust her, my stomach still lurches as she unzips my backpack and opens it up. All of my school books are in there, a few pencils, two notebooks.

And my laptop.

"Do you need this computer for class?" Mom's hand rests lightly on the laptop as she waits for my response.

I have to drag my eyes away from her hand and look her in the eyes. "No."

"Well, then do you think it might be a better idea to leave it here so you don't have to worry about anything happening to it at school?" She waits for me to answer, crouched perfectly still, almost like she's doing everything in her power to keep from scaring me.

"Nothing will happen to it here," she tells me. "I promise. I lock the door when I leave and it'll be safer here than at school."

Finally, I nod. I know she's right. Of course she's right.

I trust her.

It's just that the last thing I want is for her to know what I've done.

19

ZOE

My phone rings when I'm halfway across town. At first, I don't answer it. When the number pops up on my screen and I don't recognize it, my knee-jerk reaction is to press the red decline button and move on with my morning.

Telemarketers, am I right?

But maybe it's someone from Micah's school calling from a personal phone and he's in trouble. If the main school line were tied up for some reason then it's not beyond the realm of possibility that a staff member would use their personal phone to try to get in touch with me, especially if there was a big problem. The last thing I want is for him to think he can't trust me, not when I've been doing everything I can to make him see how safe he is at our house.

So I pick up.

"Hello? This is Zoe," I say, trying my best to sound busy, but friendly.

"Zoe Steele? This is Greta from the police station, calling to touch base about our discussion yesterday."

"Greta, hi, thanks so much for calling me back." I hesitate. Should I tell her that I'm on my way to Micah's old house right now to check in on things? No, probably not. From watching the news and reading the paper I've learned that police don't like it when you second-guess them about anything. Best to let them think I'm one hundred percent behind how they're handling their job.

"Do you have a moment?"

"Of course. What can I do for you?"

She sighs. "We sent Officer Barnwell to the address you gave him yesterday after he stopped by to talk to Micah, but there was no sign of anyone home. We'll send someone back today, but as far as we can tell, Rita wasn't there."

My heart pounds in my chest. See? This is why it's a good thing I'm willing to drive out there. The police probably drove slowly by the house, peering out the window, munching on a donut at the same time. I doubt they even got out of the car to poke around. I'm willing to look in windows and talk to neighbors.

"Well, I appreciate you looking into it," I say.

At that moment, my GPS pipes up, telling me to turn on Brookdale.

Crap. Did she hear where I'm going? Would she even care?

"Do you have any other information on Rita? A phone number? Place of employment?"

"No, I'm sorry, I don't." My stomach sinks. If they can't easily find her and I don't have any proof of her being alive in the first place, then what's that mean for Micah?

It means he stays with us, that's what it means.

"Well, you have a good day, then. Do get in contact with us if you have any other information you wish to share. We'll keep an eye out for Rita, but it's a bit of a dead end right now."

Speaking of dead ends... I gently press the brake as I pull into a driveway on the cul-de-sac.

"Thank you, Greta," I say. "I'll talk to you later." And I hang up.

Stare at the house in front of me.

No way.

There's no freaking way.

I don't know much about Rita—or Micah, for that matter —but there's no way this was where they lived. Flowers in full bloom—without a weed in sight—line the brick walkway that leads up to the wide front porch. There are rocking chairs as well as more potted plants on the porch. Hanging ferns give it a welcoming feel.

Slowly, like I'm doing something illegal, I get out of my car and walk up to the garage. Everyone on the street has windows in their garage, their blank reflections facing the street, but some people have hung curtains to keep nosy people from looking in. Cupping my hands around my eyes, I exhale with relief when I see these windows are curtainless.

There's a car sitting in the garage. Not a BMW or anything, but a car, nonetheless. Probably something with reasonable gas mileage and good trunk space, from the looks of it.

So someone is home. Or they were, at least. I smooth down my shirt and glance around at the other houses on the cul-de-sac. It's early and everyone must be at work, because there isn't any movement on the street.

But maybe someone is home. Rita. Maybe Rita is home.

Maybe Micah lied about everything. That thought works

its way into my mind and settles down, making it difficult for me to think of anything else. If this is where Micah grew up, in this gorgeous home with perfectly manicured lawns all the way down the street, I highly doubt a neighbor wouldn't have noticed the power was out.

That his mom was missing.

That things were as bad as he keeps claiming them to be.

So what's the alternative?

"The alternative, Zoe, is that you're going to knock on the door and Rita's going to open it. The police missed her yesterday because she was still at work but maybe she got a late start this morning. Maybe she's been scouring Facebook looking for any proof of her son having walked away from home. Maybe she got in this morning from a business trip and can't find Micah."

Bolstered by that thought—that this was all a big misunderstanding—I walk purposefully to the front porch. There's a cup of tea sitting by one of the rocking chairs and I note with pleasure that it's still steaming.

Yeah, someone's here.

I feel the triumphant smile on my face as I press the doorbell, then step back, wanting to make sure Rita can see me before she opens the door. The chimes tinkle in the house, a song instead of a random tune, and I dust my hands on my pants.

This ends now. Whatever's going on, wherever Rita was, whatever mental problems Micah must have to lie to me about how his mother treated him, it's all over now.

The door swings open and I smile wider, wanting to make sure I look as non-threatening as possible. That's key, when stopping by someone's house unannounced. You don't want to look like a threat.

The woman who joins me on the porch looks about my age. She has perfectly coiffed black hair pulled back into a tight bun, light makeup, and a dancer's body. She eyes me warily, then gestures for me to join her in a rocking chair.

For a moment I consider it. "No, thank you. I wanted to stop by and talk to you, Rita. I'm Zoe. Ethan's wife."

Nothing. No sign of recognition. If anything, she frowns at me.

"I'm sorry, who?" There's a soft accent when she speaks. "I'm not Rita. I'm Louisa. I got back into town late last night and I'm a little tired, so you have to forgive me. Who are you looking for?"

Heat flushes my cheeks. "Rita. I'm looking for Rita. I was told she lives here. Micah told me?"

"Micah?" She shakes her head. "I'm so sorry, I have no idea who that is."

My stomach sinks. I honestly thought I'd figured everything out. It wasn't going to be pleasant to reconcile Micah as a liar and to explain that to Ethan, but I was willing to do it if that's what it took to get to the bottom of this.

When I pulled up into the driveway I'd thought for sure he'd lied, that maybe he'd struggled with his mom's work schedule, that he'd decided to research his dad and come to us rather than dealing with the rules of his house. That maybe he specifically chose the worst possible clothes to wear so we'd feel bad for him.

But if he lied to me then no wonder he has such a nice laptop.

I take a deep breath, squeezing my hands into fists before forcing myself to relax them. I need to calm down.

"You don't know Micah or Rita?" I ask, to make sure I heard her correctly. "You're sure about that?"

"I promise you," she tells me, lifting her chin a little, "I've never met either of them. Now, if you'll excuse me..." Her voice trails off because she's being polite, but it's clear what she wants.

I nod. Turn around. Stalk back to my car.

On the inside, though, I'm shaking. I don't want her to see it, don't want to admit it to anyone, but I'm terrified.

Who the hell did I let into my house?

20

ZOE

Dinner is spaghetti. The pot bubbles on the stove and I stir it slowly, not in a hurry to speed things up. Anna's at the table behind me drawing and Micah's in his room working on homework. As soon as Ethan gets back from work, he and I have some things to talk about, but he's running behind tonight.

That's nothing new. It happens from time to time. A patient might need a little extra attention, or maybe checking on his surgical patients from the morning is taking longer than normal.

Footsteps behind me tell me that Micah's joined us in the kitchen and I turn around right as he speaks.

"Hey, Mom? Do you mind if I take Anna outside to play?" He's wearing more of the clothes I bought him and he tugs at the hem of his blue t-shirt. "It's nice out and I wanted to show her where this cool toad I found was living."

I hesitate. It should be an easy answer, shouldn't it? I should feel totally comfortable telling him to take her outside and play until dinner's ready, but I can't seem to form the words. "It's almost dinner," I begin.

But Anna pipes up. "I want to go outside with my brudder!"

Micah's face lights up.

Behind me on the stove I hear the boiling water pop and hiss, and I turn to stir it. The scraping of chair legs on the floor tells me Anna's on the move.

"Outside! Outside! Outside!" It's a chant now and she points at Micah, getting him to join in.

"Outside!" He grins at her and then turns to look at me. "Outside! Outside!"

They're in unison now, their voices so loud it's impossible for me to think straight. My heart beats faster and I feel the beginnings of a migraine. There's pressure right behind my eyes, and it's growing, like someone inserted an ice pick right there. "Fine, go," I say, throwing my hands up in the air. "Go, but stay close to the house, understand? I need to be able to look out the windows and see you."

Pointing to the front windows, I give Micah a hard look.

"Of course. The toad is right there by the house. Don't worry, Mom, I won't let anything happen to Anna." He reaches out and takes her hand and she slips her fingers into his.

So willing. So trusting, I think, and watch as the two of them race out the front door.

"Deep breaths," I tell myself, turning back to the stove. If I'm not careful, dinner's going to burn, and I turn off the flame, giving the spaghetti one more stir before checking my phone for a message from Ethan.

Where is he?

I'm about to call him when I hear the familiar rumble of

his car in the driveway. Rushing to the window, I lift the blind and look out. True to his word, Micah and Anna are crouched near the house. I watch as they wave at Ethan and then turn their attention back to whatever's on the ground between them.

My hands shake as I pour Ethan a glass of whiskey, the amber liquid seeming to glow in the cut glass. By the time he opens the door from the garage I'm there, pressing the drink into his hand.

"This is a lovely way to be greeted," he tells me, drawing me in for a kiss before taking a sip of his drink. "Tell me, what's the occasion?"

"I wanted to talk to you while the kids are outside," I say, reaching for his empty travel mug and depositing it in the sink. By the time I make it back to him, he's already kicked off his shoes and is shrugging out of his jacket. I help him, then follow him to the living room.

"Is everything okay?" He sits down on the leather sofa he bought with his first paycheck from the hospital and I hover nearby before settling next to him. I hate this sofa, if I'm being honest. It looks like something you'd find in a shrink's office, but Ethan loves it.

He says it makes him feel like he finally made it.

"It's fine," I say, but then change my mind. "Kinda. I went to the address Micah gave me today to see if I could find any sign of Rita, any proof of where she went, but the woman living there told me she's never heard of Rita."

Ethan stares at me. He blinks, slowly, like he's having trouble taking in everything I'm saying.

"It was a gorgeous home," I continue, almost tripping over my words in an effort to make him understand what's on my mind. "Not at all like what Micah told us about. But he didn't live there. Why would he say that was his address?"

Ethan takes a sip. I watch as he swirls the liquid around in his mouth before swallowing. When he speaks, our faces are close enough I can smell the whiskey on his breath.

"Do you think he lied?"

I don't know. Now would be the perfect time to come clean about the photograph he doctored up, but I can't seem to make myself say the words. Why is that? Why am I too afraid to tell my husband about the one thing that sent me spiraling down this path of not believing Micah?

I think I know.

Micah's his son. He's a reflection on Ethan, whether or not we like it. Just like Ethan's been worried what people in town will say about him having a child he didn't even know about, I guess I'm worried about what Ethan will say or do if he finds out Micah isn't completely honest.

And what it will mean for us if that's true.

He'll be angry at Micah, I know he will. Ethan will want to kick him out of the house, and while that would make things easier on me, it wouldn't solve anything.

Not really.

Sure, Micah would be gone, but he'd still be having problems. The kid is messed up, but that doesn't mean he's dangerous, right? It means he needs help. Therapy, probably. If he's not in our house, would anyone get him the help he needs?

"I don't know," I say, rather than voicing any of my other concerns. "Do you think that's a possibility?"

"Sure, lying is always a possibility." He takes another sip of his whiskey and levels his gaze at me. "Or it could be something not nearly as insidious."

"Like?"

"Like he got mixed up. Like he's been through more trauma in his life than we could ever begin to understand and he forgot his correct address when talking to you. I know we want everything to be cut and dry, Zoe, but sometimes people make mistakes."

But not Ethan. He doesn't make mistakes. Not in his marriage, not at work.

"Maybe," I say, but I'm not entirely convinced. "It felt weird, that's all. To drive all the way over there and then have the woman look at me like I was crazy. I felt like I was in a bad movie or something."

This makes him laugh. "I think what you're doing, inviting Micah in and taking care of him, has got to be stressful. More so than I thought at first, if I'm being honest. I love you for it, Zoe."

"I love you," I say, and I mean it. That's a big part of why I felt like we couldn't turn Micah away. He's part of Ethan. Sure, he's a part of my husband I didn't know until recently, but he's still part of Ethan. And that's important to me.

"Oh, and related but not, I talked to Bonnie." Ethan grins at me. Swirls his drink. Drains the glass. "It went swimmingly. You were right."

"Excellent." Taking his glass I stand, then motion for him to follow me into the kitchen. "So she's spreading the information about Micah being your son and what a great guy you are helping the kid out and you didn't have to even lift a finger?"

He laughs. "Basically." While I pour him a drink, he wanders over to the stove and stirs the spaghetti. "Shall I call the kids in for dinner? Maybe we can get them to bed early and finally watch that movie we've been wanting to see."

"Sounds like a plan." Inspired now, I put his drink on the table and plate our food. In addition to the spaghetti, we're having garlic bread and salads. The kids both get water and I'm having some wine. If I don't pass out halfway during the movie, it will be a surprise, but the day has been so long all I want is something to take the edge off.

And wine is the perfect thing for it.

I want to believe the best of Micah. I do. That's part of the reason why I didn't tell Ethan about the photograph.

But the other reason is because I was the one who was completely on board with Micah moving into the house and becoming part of the family. Ethan was the one dragging his feet, worried about his reputation, worried about upsetting the balance in the house.

If I express my concerns about Micah to Ethan, what will happen if my husband thinks the boy needs to go? Sure, now that word has gotten out that he has another son and nobody is coming for him with pitchforks, maybe he'd be willing to let Micah stay.

But what if not?

I won't be the reason this boy loses another home.

There has to be a logical explanation for everything that's been going on.

21

MICAH

I know I was supposed to be in bed a while ago, but the soft glow of my laptop's screen fills my room as I connect to the internet and navigate to Facebook.

I'm *too young* to have a Facebook account, or that's what their terms of use say, but who actually reads and follows those? I know that I don't, not when having an account might get me what I want.

And what I want is any sign that someone has found my mom. Knows what's happened to her. Has any idea of the truth of where she is.

My fingers tremble as I log in, then navigate to the local yard sale site. It's ludicrous, that a yard sale group could become the hot spot for news on Facebook, but that's exactly what's happened here. It started out as a place to sell unwanted items, but more and more people post random things.

Lost dogs.

Accident reports.

Possible Bigfoot sightings.

Missing persons.

That's what I'm most interested in, and I type my mom's name in the search bar, then click enter. The internet here is super-fast and it only takes a moment for the search to come back.

No results.

Well then, what about a body? If someone had found a body then the little old biddies in this group would surely be talking about it. They love drama—not only theirs, but anyone else's they can stir up.

Body.

Now I have some results, but none of them are what I'm looking for. Body suits. Body wax. Full body massage.

I frown and click back to the main page, then type in a new search.

Zoe Steele.

There she is. My new mom, smiling at me from her Facebook page, her arms flung wide, hiking boots on her feet and a great view of the mountains behind her.

I scroll through her timeline, looking for anything recent she's uploaded.

No posts about me.

There's footsteps in the hall and I panic, clicking the little X in the corner of the browser to make it disappear. Then, before I'm caught, I close my laptop and slide it under my covers, flopping down on the bed next to it and yanking the sheet up to my chin.

A soft knock, then the door opens.

"Hey, Micah, you good?" It's Zoe. Her words are a little slurred, like she had more than one glass of wine with dinner. She leans against the doorframe in pink pajamas and she looks so pretty it takes me a moment to answer.

"I'm fine," I say, then force a yawn. "Just getting comfortable."

"Right. Good." She raps her knuckles against the door-frame. "If you need us, we're right next door. I'll see you in the morning."

I nod. "Goodnight."

"Night, Micah." She closes the door softly behind her, but I wait until I hear her footsteps disappear down the hall to exhale in relief.

I don't know what she'd say if she caught me on the computer right now. She'd want to know what I was doing, what I was looking at.

And I don't want to tell her.

It's silly, because I haven't been here that long, but I already know one thing.

This place is a lot better than my old home and there's no way I'm going to leave.

22

ZOE

Friday March 17

Micah was on his laptop last night. I'm sure of it.

Did I catch him?

No, not technically.

But I saw the guilt written all over his face, like he was doing something he most certainly shouldn't. I guess I could have pushed it, could have demanded that he let me see what he was doing on his computer, and maybe that's what another parent—a *better* parent—would have done in my situation.

I didn't do that and now the moment is gone. Rather than asking him what he was doing and putting him on the defensive, I'm going to find out on my own. No, it probably isn't sanctioned for me to do this. I'm sure a lot of mommy bloggers would take umbrage with what I'm about to do.

But they're not here to stop me, are they?

Still, I feel nervous as I walk up the stairs and turn down the hall to his bedroom. It's right next to ours, away from Anna's, just in case, but it still feels like I'm walking into another country when I push open his door and step inside. I move hesitantly, almost like I'm expecting some sort of homemade booby-traps like in *Home Alone*.

But I don't walk into any tripwires. Nothing swings down from the ceiling, aiming for my face. There aren't any alarms or sirens that sound, not that I expected any.

It's strange being in his space without his knowledge. Without his permission.

Now that I'm here, though, I feel more confident about what I'm doing. I walk with purpose over to the desk Ethan set up for Micah, right under the window, so he can look out into the yard while working on his homework. There's a stack of paper on the desk along with a stray pencil, but when I lift it, the laptop isn't anywhere to be found.

So where is it?

Surely he didn't take it with him to school today, right? The absurdity of him doing that on the day I venture up here is enough to make me want to scream.

No, I don't think he'd do that. Not after we had our conversation yesterday about how much safer it would be here, at the house, where nobody could steal it from him when his back was turned.

Of course, I don't want to think about how I waited until his back was turned to take advantage of him trusting me. That thought bothers me, making me feel guilty, and I push it away as I open his closet door.

Messy. Exactly like I expected. I'd probably smile about that, at the fact that he's a textbook teenage boy, but I'm more irritated than anything else. Messy will make it harder for me to find what I'm looking for. And although I'm not on a time crunch, I still feel the pressure to find the laptop, to open it and dig through it, then to hide it back away before I pick him up from school.

There's a pile of dirty clothes on the floor of his closet and I toe it to the side.

No laptop.

On a shelf, then? Under a sweater I bought him in case it got chilly one morning before school?

Nope.

Not in the closet, then. After closing the door behind me I walk back to his bed and drop to my knees, peering under it for any sign of his electronics. There are a pair of shoes as well as a pair of slippers I bought him for wearing around the house.

But no laptop.

"Where did you put it, you sneaky kid?" I ask, standing and turning in a slow circle. There aren't a lot of other places for him to hide it. No, scratch that. I can't think of *any* other places for him to hide it if he wanted to keep it in his room, and I doubt he'd put it somewhere else.

Right as I'm about to leave, I remember that he'd been in bed on it last night when I saw him.

Maybe...

Excitement courses through me as I grab his coverlet and yank it back. He made his bed this morning, but it was sloppily done, so I'm not worried about him being able to tell I was in here messing with it.

Nothing under the coverlet.

But there is a lump under the sheet.

Bingo.

Almost frantic now, I tug the sheet back and grab the

laptop, sitting down and opening it in one fluid motion. My hands shake a bit and I take a deep breath to calm my nerves before tapping the enter key.

No password. Either he doesn't know enough to try to keep his stuff safe and locked down, or he never worried about it before.

I'd wager it's the latter.

There are a few saved Word files on his desktop and I click through them. Poetry, mostly.

"Bad poetry," I whisper. That's a rite of passage for any teenager, isn't it? I know I wrote more than my fair share of it when I was younger.

Some pictures he's obviously saved from online. Celebrities, mostly skinny models in lingerie on catwalks. I don't love the thought of him looking at pictures like this when he's still a kid, but I don't see a way I can stop it, not without causing a scene. Besides, it's normal. I might not like it, but it's normal.

There are also a few folders on his desktop and I open the first one, pleased to see it's full of papers he worked on for school. Good, good. Closing it, I open the second. Some articles he's saved from online. I skim through them, not wanting to get bogged down in what he found important enough to save, but still curious.

There are a few on owning a dog for the first time. One on how to be a big brother.

Well then, maybe he's been doing some research on how to make his life into what he wants it to be. It's heartwarming, honestly. The thought of him up here, under his covers, trying to figure out how to be the best person he can, how to fit into this family, how to take care of a dog sometime in the future... I like it.

I'm smiling as I close the folder and open the last one.

The smile slips from my face.

I know these pictures. I've seen them before, although some of them are so old I honestly forgot that they'd ever been taken. Still, even though I hadn't seen them in a while, there's no way I wouldn't recognize them.

Because they're all of me.

23

ZOE

My breath catches in my throat as I click through the folder. It's like going back in time, slowly working my way backwards from now to when I was younger and first had an online presence. There are pictures of me at charity events, some of me at Anna's preschool.

A photo of Ethan and me when he cut the ribbon at a new wing in the hospital.

Ones before I ever got pregnant, snapshots that made it into the local paper for various events he was invited to. I remember going to those events, remember how I'd down a glass of wine as soon as we got there to try to calm my nerves. I remember the fancy dresses we'd buy so I'd look my best.

They're still in the back of my closet.

My heart is in my throat as I click through the pictures. I keep getting younger. Some of them are of both Ethan and me, although more and more of them are me by myself. Me in college. Me graduating high school.

He must have been looking for a long time to find these. I can't imagine that he discovered all of these over the past few nights that he's been at the house.

My hands are sweaty and I wipe my palms on my jeans before right clicking on a picture file and opening the file's info. A lot of it doesn't mean anything to me and isn't important to what I'm looking for, but then I see it.

The date the file was created on his computer.

"No," I whisper, pushing the laptop off my lap onto the bed next to me like I'm afraid it's going to bite me. I stare at the screen, stare at the numbers there like looking them head-on is going to be enough to make them change, but they don't change.

The truth is written there in black and white. Computers don't lie.

Micah saved this one picture to his computer over two months ago.

The reality of what that means—that he'd been looking me up for a long time now—makes me feel like I'm choking. I close out of the info and select another photo, going through the same steps to find out how long it's existed on his computer.

Three months.

Four.

My movements are jerky, frantic. I knock into the laptop and it slips to the side, almost tipping over the edge of the bed to land on the floor, but I grab it at the last moment, pulling it back up onto my lap and holding it there with both hands.

It's become both the most precious and vile thing to me. Precious because it has answers I never knew I was looking for, and vile because I don't like what I'm finding.

There's only one more thing to do right now. I glance down at the time on the screen. It feels like I've been looking in Micah's computer for an eternity but it's only been about ten minutes. Taking a deep breath, I open his browser and go to the history tab.

I have to know what else he's been looking for.

Me, obviously. He's been looking for me. And there are some articles he's saved to his desktop that make his internet searches look innocent. Cute, almost. But I doubt, having seen what he has saved in his little folders on his desktop, that the rest of his internet searches are going to be nearly as innocent.

"You can do this," I say, pepping myself up to open the history tab. Finally, I click it, the rows of text filling the screen. Moving quickly, I skim the list, looking for anything that sticks out, anything that I should be aware of immediately.

Lots of internet searches for his new school. His teacher. Some of his classmates. Looks like he checked out their Facebook profiles but didn't leave any comments.

Farther back, then. Before I even knew he existed. My fingers are cramped from how I'm holding them to swipe the trackpad and I take a moment, shaking them out before continuing.

What happens if your mom disappears?

When do you assume your mom is dead?

Does your biological dad have to let you live with him?

My blood runs cold. I swear, it feels like a chill has

descended on my body, like my breath is trapped in my lungs. I try to take a deep breath to get rid of the feeling of unease, but I can't seem to get my lungs to expand.

Just existing hurts.

Breathing hurts.

My head pounds and I close out of the browser, carefully shut Micah's laptop, then remake his bed, taking care to ensure the computer is exactly where I found it earlier. The last thing I want is for him to have any inkling I was in his room.

What has he been planning?

It feels like my vision is blurry as I grab my phone and tap at the screen to dial Ethan's number. I know he's in surgery—he always likes to operate in the morning so he can see patients in the afternoon before coming home—but I have to talk to him. Even though interrupting him is the one thing I've never wanted to do, I don't see that I have a choice in the matter right now.

He has to know what's going on. It's only fair.

One ring. Two. On the third I'm starting to sweat, wondering if maybe this was a mistake, if I should wait for him to come home so we can talk, then there's a click and Bonnie's voice fills my ear.

"Zoe, what a surprise. What can I do for you?"

"Hi, Bonnie." I swallow hard, doing my best to keep my voice as even and calm as possible. "I know Ethan's probably in surgery but I need to talk to him."

"Is it an emergency?" There's a squeak as she moves in her chair, getting as comfortable as possible for any gossip she can lap up, I'd wager. "Is there a problem with Micah? Dr. Steele told me all about him, the poor little lamb. So good of Ethan to open his doors to the boy, even though I understand why you were a bit reticent."

It isn't lost on me that Ethan spun the truth of how Micah came to live with us to ensure he looked as good as possible, but I don't want to get into that with Bonnie right now.

I grit my teeth. "Micah's fine, Bonnie, thank you so much for asking. But please, I need to talk to Ethan."

"Let me go see who he's operating with." Another squeak and now I hear the sound of her heels on the tile floor. "If he has Dr. Lynn in there then I'm sure he can pop out and talk to you. Are you sure there isn't something I can do to help you?"

"I'm sure." I'm up now, pacing in Micah's room. Even though I know moving around isn't going to help me deal with the problem at hand, I don't want to sit still. I don't like the thought of waiting for something to happen to me—I want to be in control of what's happening.

"Well, I wanted to offer. You know, it's always best, as wives, if we can try to handle things on our own instead of roping our husbands in to handle the problem. Men appreciate that, Zoe."

"I'm sure they do." My cheeks hurt from smiling but it's the only way I can keep from screaming at the woman. As much as I hate to admit it, if I lose my cool with Bonnie, she will make my life a living hell. I don't know how she gained the confidence of every doctor at the hospital, but she has.

Even when I was a nurse there, she was in charge of everything. She knows all, sees all, and has dirt on everyone. It's great when she's on your side, but not so great when you're at her mercy.

"Well, you're in luck. He's not in there alone, and Dr. Lynn is more than able to handle finishing up. I'm going to put you down, Zoe, so don't hang up. As long as Dr. Steele isn't too preoccupied to talk with you, he'll be here in a minute."

There's a thunk as she puts the phone down on a counter or table, then silence.

I keep pacing, pausing from time to time to look out of Micah's window. Each time I do, I have to brush the curtain to the side to see out and I wonder if any neighbors are watching me. They'll wonder what I'm doing, they'll wonder—

"Zoe?" Ethan's worried. I hear it in his voice. "Is something wrong?"

"Ethan, I have to tell you something," I say, but an insistent beep in my ear makes me pause. "Crap, someone is calling me. Hang on a moment. I'm so sorry, Ethan, I know you're busy."

Exhaling hard, I pull the phone from my ear and look at the screen. When Anna started preschool I promised myself —and her—that I wouldn't ever ignore a phone call when she was away from me, on the off chance she needed me. This is probably nothing.

A telemarketer. They always seem to know the best worst time to call, right when you don't have the time or energy to deal with them. Surely that's all this is.

But it's not. A chill washes over me when I look at the phone, at the name there, the screen lit up and insistent, telling me that I better pick up the call as soon as possible, before something terrible happens.

It's Micah's school and, for the life of me, I can't think of a single good reason why they'd be calling.

24

ZOE

I tell Ethan I'll call him back even though right now I'm bursting to tell him everything that's going on with Micah.

The photo.

The internet searches and saved photos on his computer.

And I want to talk again about Micah lying about where he lived.

All of it adds up to something much more dark, much more sinister than I ever considered when I invited him to live with us. Had I known...

Nope, not going to go down that path. Especially not right now, not as I press the button on my phone's screen to answer the call from his school. I feel like I'm close to the edge, like I'm honestly about to fall apart, but I plaster a smile on my face when I answer.

Isn't that what women are always taught to do? Fake a smile when you speak and nobody will ever be able to tell that you're completely falling apart. It's messed up, that's what it is, but it works.

And so we keep doing it.

"Hello?" I sound confident. In control.

Not at all like I've just learned that my husband's son is more messed up than I ever could have thought.

"Mrs. Steele? This is Rebecca Jacobs, the nurse at East Middle. I'm calling about Micah."

"Of course." I clear my throat. One hand holds the phone up to my ear, the other is spread on my thigh, my nails digging through my pants into my skin. "What can I do for you? Is he okay?"

"He doesn't feel well," she tells me, and I hear the concern in her voice. "He has a stomachache and said that he thought he might throw up."

"Oh, no." *Oh, no, indeed.* "Does he have a fever? I'm trying to remember what he ate for breakfast, but I don't think anyone else in our house is feeling ill."

"No fever, but he was pretty insistent that he felt sick. I hate to bother you at home when I'm sure you have things going on, but he can't go back to class if he's going to be a disruption."

"Of course not. Can he sit in your office until I come get him?"

"He's welcome to stay for a bit, but I will need the cot in case anyone else starts to feel ill. Thank you for making coming to get him a priority."

Translation: yes, he can stay with me for a bit, but you better not lollygag because I have other things to do than look after him and keep him from throwing up.

"I understand that." I look around his room. How likely is it that he'd have any idea that I was in here? I don't think he'll be able to tell. "Let me finish up what I'm doing here and I'll head right over."

I feel discombobulated, like I can't think straight. I've been thrown for a loop and now I won't even have the time I want to try to think things through. Rather than getting to work through what's going on, I'm going to go get Micah.

I'll have to talk to him and pretend everything is fine even though I know it's not.

"Sounds great, Mrs. Steele. I'll see you soon. Goodbye."

"Goodbye," I respond, but she's already hung up. Like I'm on autopilot, I walk out of the room and down the hall. For a moment, I stand outside Anna's room.

Should I put a lock on her door to keep her safe while Micah is here?

No, he'd be able to reach up and undo it. There's no way to lock her in without him being able to unlock the door.

Should I lock him in his room?

"Oh, my God." I press my fingers against my mouth as I consider what I was thinking. Of course I can't lock him in his room. He's a kid! What if there were an emergency, like a fire? What then, if he needed to get out of his room and he couldn't?

No, that's not an option.

I have no memory of walking down the stairs, but suddenly I'm in the car, backing out of the garage. When I pull out of the driveway I press the little phone button on my steering wheel.

"Call Ethan," I announce. It's more important than ever to let him know what's going on. I'll tell him everything, starting at the beginning with the photo. No, with how strange it is for Micah to call me *Mom*. I'll tell him about the photo, the pictures, the internet history, the—

"You can't stay away, can you, Zoe?" Bonnie's laughing

like we're good friends, like she was sitting around waiting for my call.

"Hi, Bonnie." I turn onto the main road, match the speed of traffic. "I'm sorry to call back, but I need to talk to Ethan. Is he available?"

"He said you might call back, but that he couldn't take your call. Back-to-back surgeries, you know. It's got to be hard to be so popular." She laughs. "But I'll leave him a note and let him know you called. Again."

"Don't worry about it," I say, drumming my fingers on the steering wheel. If she does that and Ethan calls when I'm with Micah, there's no way I'll be able to tell him the truth of what's going on. "I'll catch him after work, Bonnie, thanks."

She's saying something but I hang up on her. Stop at a red light.

Who can I talk to?

As the light turns green, it hits me. The police officer. Barnwell. He made it clear when he stopped by that I could call about anything, at any time. Surely someone has gone by the address Micah gave me by now and learned what I have—that he lied about ever living there.

Surely that will be enough to make the police a little more curious about what's going on with the boy.

I pull into the school parking lot and turn off the car, then grab my purse and start digging through it for the officer's business card. I know he gave it to me. My fingers fumble through the detritus of my purse. There are receipts, gum wrappers, five pens, a baggie of goldfish, my wallet, two tampons, my phone, and a handful of paperclips.

But no business card.

I must have dropped it somewhere.

"I'll call the department," I say, grabbing my phone and

tapping the screen. It lights up immediately and I shoot a guilty glance at the phone as I dial the non-emergency number. I need to hurry it up and get Micah.

But this won't take long.

"Greenbriar Police Department. This is Richard. How can I help you?"

"Richard, hi. This is Zoe Steele. I need to talk to Officer Barnwell. Is he working today?"

A pause, then, "No, ma'am, Officer Barnwell is off this weekend, but will be back Monday. Do you want to leave a message for him?"

"No, I... He was at my house the other day to talk to my son. Well, my husband's son. His mom is missing and I wanted to talk through something I thought of."

"I can have another officer give you a ring. But they're all out on calls right now, and if this isn't an emergency then it will move to the back of the queue."

Of course it will. "I guess that's fine," I say, even though it isn't. "Oh, wait! Do you know if anyone drove by his house yesterday? They went Wednesday night but nobody was there. Greta told me about it."

"Greta isn't working today either," he tells me. There's a tone to his voice and I can't tell if he's frustrated with me or the situation. "Mrs. Steele, the best thing is to wait for an officer to give you a call back. They'll have more information for you."

"Right, thank you. I'll wait then." Before he can say anything else, I hang up. Mature? Definitely not. Did it feel good though? Yes, yes, it did.

Now that that call is over and I didn't get any more information than when I started out, I tuck my phone into my purse and walk up to the school. I'm nervous, which is silly on one level. It's not that I've been called a lot of times to pick Anna up from preschool because she was sick, but enough that I know the protocol for the preschool, and it's probably the same for Micah's school.

No, the problem isn't that I'm going to be dealing with a sick kid.

The problem is dealing with Micah.

The front door is locked and I press a buzzer to be let in. At the front office I tell the girl working who I am and that the nurse called. Her face, a little sunburned from too much time outside, lights up.

"Oh, good. We love it when parents come by as quickly as possible to pick up their kids. He'll be so glad to see you. The nurse told me he was asking for his mom." She points down the hall. "Second door on the right."

I don't have the heart to tell her I'm not Micah's biological mom. What good would it do in the long run? If she doesn't know what's going on in my family, then why tell her? It would only open us up to more gossip. And, if what Ethan told me is true, he's got it under control.

Everyone will know the truth eventually. There's no reason to rush it.

That is, if Micah stays with us.

That thought echoes in my head as I walk down the hall, my shoes loud on the squeaky clean tile. At the second door on the right I pause, then give a little knock as I push it open, revealing a small nurse's office.

A woman sits at a desk, her back to me. *Rebecca, I'm assuming.* She turns when she hears the door open, a smile spreading across her face. Along one wall is a small cot. Micah's on it, a blanket pulled up to his chin, a small trash can next to him.

In case he throws up. Right.

He looks... well, fine. He looks fine. He looks like any other kid right now. His cheeks are a normal color, not flushed like he has a fever, not pale like he's going to be sick. He honestly seems completely and totally fine and the thought that he might have pulled one over on me frustrates me.

"Hi, Mom." Micah sits up, a grin spreading across his face. "You came."

"Of course I came," I say, still standing in the door. I should go to him. Should comfort him. Should do *something* to try to make him feel better, but I don't feel like I can move.

That's fine, though, because he gets up and comes to me, wrapping his arms around me. I pat his back, my mind racing as I try to work through my emotions. If he's not sick and he called me here because he missed me, I should be upset. I *am* upset, but not angry.

I'm more heartbroken for him than anything else.

"You're a better mother than she ever was," he breathes, leaning harder into me.

I swell with pride, pleased that I can be that person for him, pleased that I can take care of him in the way he needs and hasn't ever gotten. He's troubled, yes. But he's had a hard life and hopefully now it's a little easier.

A better mother. That's me. His arms are still around me and I absently stroke his back, thinking. Thinking about what he would do if I weren't here to come get him. Would Rita have come to the school for her son? He's so grateful to me right now that I can't help but imagine she wouldn't.

Thinking about her makes my breath catch in my throat.

What really happened to Rita?

25

MICAH

Mom's silent during the drive home. She gave me a plastic bag from the backseat, one from the nice grocery store so it's a little thicker than others might be, and asked me to please aim for the bag if I get sick.

But that's it. Other than that, she's been silent.

I keep my eyes on the road. Each little bump makes my stomach twist and while I don't think I'm going to throw up, I don't feel well. I could have stayed at school. Or I could go home with Mom. It felt like a good idea at the time, like we'd get to skip school together and have some alone time without anyone else around.

But now she doesn't seem to want me here.

We pull into the garage and she pushes the button for the door to close behind us. It does with a rattle, and the garage goes dark.

"Why don't you head up to bed?" she finally asks, opening her door so the overhead light turns on.

This isn't working out the way I want it to.

"I'd rather be with you," I say, even though I'm a little embarrassed at confessing it. "I think I'll feel better if—"

"You'll feel better if you nap." Her words have an edge but she smiles a little to soften the blow. "Trust me. You go lie down and try to get some sleep. I'll bring a snack and if you have a fever I'll get you some medicine. What do you say to that?"

I hesitate. She's being loving and I know I should take her up on what she's offering, but there's part of me that feels like she's upset, and I don't like it. But why would she be mad at me?

Kids get sick. I didn't mean to feel ill. Sure, maybe I'm not technically sick, and certainly not bad enough to go to the doctor, but I don't feel well. I want my mom. And I thought moms were supposed to snuggle you when you're sick, let you lie on the sofa, things like that.

At least, that's what moms I've read about in books have done.

"Go on, Micah." She's still smiling. "Shoo. I'll be up in a bit. Depending on how you're feeling, I'll either load you into the car to get Anna or ask someone else to pick her up."

"I'll be fine to get Anna," I tell her. Suddenly I'm overcome with desperation. The last thing I want is for her to make me stay away from my little sister because she thinks I'm sicker than I am. "I'll be fine. I'll go lie down now and you'll see."

"Great." She reaches out like she's going to touch my arm but then her hand falls back by her side. I'm suddenly overcome with the desire of having her touch me, of getting a hug, but she's already turning away from me and getting out of the car.

For a moment I stay completely still and watch her walk

into the kitchen. Her shoulders round forward a little like she's disappointed in something, or like she's under so much pressure she can't help but let it press her down to the ground.

Did I do that?

Was me not feeling well and calling her to come get me from school the thing that made her look like she's... exhausted?

Or did she learn something she's not supposed to?

No. Not a chance. For her to have done that, she'd have to look on my laptop. And she wouldn't do that.

Right?

26

ZOE

I stand in the kitchen, my hands planted on the counter, taking deep breaths while I wait for Micah to go upstairs.

He takes his time, moving slowly, like each step is more difficult than he thought it would be. A good mother would be there with him, her arm around his shoulders, guiding him up the stairs and making sure he didn't get weak and lose his balance.

But that's the last thing I want to do right now. My head pounds and even though I know there's no possible way he gave me whatever it was making him feel sick, I don't like the way I feel lightheaded, weak, like I'm out of control.

I've never felt this way before. Even though I don't want to admit it, I know that feeling like this started when Micah moved in. *No,* not when Micah moved in.

When I started to learn more about who he really is.

He seemed like such a nice kid, and that's why I was determined to make sure he could stay here. It's not his fault that his mom left him alone at the house, that she hasn't been around, that he's had to raise himself.

Or is it?

"No, no, no, you're spiraling." I press my fingers into my temples to try to calm myself down, but it's not working. Taking a deep breath, I eyeball my purse. My phone is there, and it would be so easy to grab it and call someone. Ethan. The police.

But I can't keep bothering Ethan and apparently I need to wait for the police to call. It's crazy to me that a few days ago I was sitting here telling the police that Ethan and I had it under control, that *of course* Micah had a home with us, that it wasn't going to be any problem having him around.

But that was before I knew what I know now.

My fingers itch to open his laptop back up, to see what else he might have been hiding. Who knows what other things I might have found if I'd taken a bit more time to poke around rather than freaking out and hiding it back in his bed?

I check the clock. It's only ten, which means I still have plenty of time before I need to be at the preschool to pick up Anna. I tried to make it sound easy when talking to Micah, like it wouldn't be any big deal to have someone else pick her up for me, but things aren't quite that simple. I'd have to call and give the pickup person's name to the director then make sure they were there on time...

No, it's best if I go pick her up. I had a wonderful afternoon for the two of us planned and I can't help but feel frustrated that he's encroaching on it. I know this is something that can happen with kids, that they get sick and interrupt plans, but it feels different this time.

Sighing, I turn away from my purse and phone. There

isn't anyone I can call right now for help, not unless I want to try to go through Bonnie again. And, unfortunately, if I call Ethan one more time today she's going to think for sure we have issues. That's the last thing I want.

"So go check on him," I say to myself, but I don't move. Tilting my head back, I look up, trying to picture exactly where Micah's room is. I think he's right above me, but I've never been great with abstract thinking and spatial reasoning.

If he is right above me, that means he might be listening for me. Goosebumps break out over my arms and I rub them, then force myself to walk across the kitchen to the stairs. I told him I'd be up in a bit with a snack and some medicine.

I'm not a liar.

Do I want to go up there? No, I don't.

Am I comfortable going to see what he's doing? Not really.

But I climb the stairs anyway, my hand gripping the railing tight. At the top of the stairs I turn, looking down the hall to our rooms. Ethan's and mine is on the end with a huge attached bathroom. There's a spare room next to ours, and that's where I put Micah.

Anna's room is the second biggest, of course, because why shouldn't our child have the best room? The guest room next to hers is nicer than the one I put Micah in, but I wanted him close.

Like keeping an eye on him would prevent anything bad from happening.

His door is cracked and I keep my eyes on it as I walk down the hall. There isn't any sound coming from it, so that's good. At least he went to bed like I told him to. I honestly don't know what I'd do if I walked in and he was on his laptop.

Lose it, probably.

"Hey, Micah," I say, keeping my voice low as I rap my knuckles on the doorframe. "I'm coming to check on you. How are you feeling?" I'm trying to be polite and give him some space, and that's why I'm still in the hall, hovering outside his door. "Micah, are you sick?"

Nothing. No answer.

The light is off in his room and I step inside, giving my eyes a moment to adjust. It's dark in here with the curtains drawn. I blink into the dark, finally sliding my hand up the wall for the light switch. "Micah. I'm turning on the light. Watch your eyes."

What if he's *really* sick? Suddenly all the worry and doubt I felt about him a moment ago sits heavy in my stomach, guilt that I might not have been there for him the way I should have been. If he's sick and I haven't supported him or if I blew it off because I didn't like how he was acting earlier, then I'm going to feel terrible.

Yes, he's creepy. But he's still a kid. From a rough background. Without any support.

I was his support and I might have made him feel like I wasn't there for him.

Guilt drives me to flick on the light without saying anything else. I'm already moving, walking over to his bed, as my eyes adjust.

But he's not there.

27

ZOE

The silence of Micah's bedroom presses down on me and even though I know what I'm seeing, even though I'm sure my eyes aren't playing tricks on me, I still can't make it make any sense.

Where in the world is he?

The room isn't very big, not by a long shot, but I still turn around slowly, wanting to make sure I didn't miss him hiding somewhere. Even as I turn, though, I know I'm not missing him.

He isn't in here.

"Micah?" My voice is louder now and I hate how nervous I sound as I call his name, but I can't help it. This doesn't make sense. He said he didn't feel well and I went to school to bring him home, for goodness' sake. So why would he tell me that, why would he go through the trouble of having me pick him up at school, why would he come up here to go to bed and then... not go to bed?

Except he didn't want to come up here, did he? He wanted to be with me. He wanted me to spend time with him until he felt better but I couldn't do that. I needed to be as far away from him as possible, no matter how terrible that sounded.

And no matter how terrible that made him feel.

"Micah, where are you?" I'm back in the hall now and maybe it's silly, but the only thing I can imagine is that he's in my room. He wanted to be close to me, didn't he?

"Micah." I walk the few steps from his door to mine and step inside. It's like night and day from his room. We have art on the wall, two huge chests of drawers for our clothes. I know it's probably decadent, but I always love having a vase full of fresh flowers in my room. It smells good in here.

Clean and floral.

But I don't see Micah.

I rush into our attached bathroom, my heart beating faster now as I race to find him. He's not in here, not hiding in the shower. Moving quickly, I open both closets and peer inside, but there's no teenage boy.

I'm back in the hall now. I can hear my heart beating in my ears as I stand there, feeling utterly useless. It's strange, to not know what to do next, to try to figure out where he might be without calling to him, but I feel like I can't speak. My tongue is too big for my mouth, too awkward, and my throat is dry.

Did he go back downstairs? I eyeball the staircase suspiciously like it should tell me all of its secrets, but I don't think he did. Sure, he can move quietly—I learned that when he first moved in with us—but surely I would have seen him on my way up.

I glance down the hall, past his room, to the bathroom.

Of course. He's in the bathroom. Who cares that the door is cracked? He's probably used to not having to close it at his old home. I can about guarantee I'm going to walk to his bathroom and peek inside and he'll be in there.

Now I feel confident as I walk down the hall and rap on the open door. "Micah, I don't want to bother you in there, but I wanted to come check on you. Can you come on out, please?"

Nothing.

I should walk into the bathroom, should check on him in there, but my eyes have fallen on another door down the hall.

One we always keep open.

One that just so happens to be closed right now.

Even though I want him to be in the bathroom—I *need* him to be in the bathroom so I can tell myself this is all a misunderstanding—I know he's not. He's not in here.

My legs are on autopilot as I walk down the hall towards the closed door. As I walk, I think about this house, how Ethan and I fell in love with it when we bought it. We laughed and talked about how wonderful it would be to fill the bedrooms with lots of kids.

Of course, we were more than willing to leave one of them empty so guests would have a place to stay when they came to visit us. Be we both wanted kids, lots of kids, bunkbeds of kids.

And, so far, it's just Anna.

"That's not entirely true, is it?" I ask myself, keeping my voice low as I walk down the hall. "You now have Micah, too."

Finally, I'm outside Anna's room. Her door is closed and I think I've solved the mystery of where Micah is but I still don't want to open the door and find out for sure. It's Schrodinger's son and he's both in her bedroom and out of her bedroom—and as long as I don't look, I don't have to know the truth.

"Micah?" His name leaves my lips in a whisper and even though I want to speak again, want to speak louder so that he'll hear me for sure this time, I can't. I just can't.

So I reach out, my fingers brushing the painted wood. I plant my hand next to the artwork Anna taped up on her door a few weeks ago, pictures of her scrawled in crayon, some of them with a dog.

A dog we don't have. The dog both of the kids living here now want.

"Micah, I'm coming."

I don't want to open the door. I don't want to know what the boy might be doing in my daughter's room, what a teenager could possibly want with a little girl's room, but there's only one way for me to find out and as much as I hate it, I have to open the door.

I have to see what he's doing.

Taking a deep breath, I turn the knob and shove the door open, my palm flat against it, pushing it hard away from me. It creaks a little as it opens—Ethan still needs to WD40 that hinge but he's so busy that I'm probably going to get tired of waiting for him to do it and do it myself—and then it's open.

And then I see Micah.

He's not even trying to hide. Not trying to hide what he's doing.

But it doesn't make any sense.

28

ZOE

I stare at Micah, slowly unsticking my tongue from the roof of my mouth. "What are you doing?"

He looks at me, his head jerking up like he's surprised to hear my voice. How he didn't hear me coming down the hall, I don't know. Each one of my steps sounded loud in my ears, like I was an elephant thundering across the ground, reverberations coming from each time my foot made contact with the floor.

"Mom." He sounds shocked and the thing he's holding slips from his hand. Anna's stuffed bunny, the one we gave her when she was born, bounces to the floor. It was purple when she got it, a pretty purple, almost lilac, but three years of being loved and dragged behind her everywhere she goes has made it more of a gray.

"Why are you in Anna's room?" I sag against the doorway as I wait for him to answer. There's part of me relieved that he's not doing anything terrible in here, nothing so bad I'd have to call Ethan and beg Bonnie to put me through before begging my husband to take it all back, to reverse my decision, to refuse to let Micah stay with us.

But if he's not doing anything wrong, not doing anything creepy, then what the hell is he doing?

"I missed her." He lifts his chin as he speaks. "And I didn't feel well."

"So you came into her room?"

"To get a stuffed animal." He gestures to the bunny on the floor. "I've never had one."

What? I can't seem to wrap my mind around what he's saying because none of it makes any sense. For a moment, I stare at him, my mind working overtime as I try to think through what to say next.

"You never had a stuffed animal, so you snuck into Anna's room to steal hers?"

"I didn't sneak." He stands, his nostrils flaring. His hands are clenched into fists by his side but when I glance down at them, he forces himself to relax. "I didn't sneak, Mom," he says, his voice softer. "I came upstairs and knew I wouldn't be able to sleep so I came in here. I miss her. And I wanted to hold her bunny."

Okay. Okay, okay. I can work with this. Or, at least I think I can.

"Alright, Micah," I say, finally stepping into the bedroom. "Would you like a stuffed animal for when you go lie down? Because I think that's a good idea right now, especially if you don't feel well. Sometimes we do and say things we wouldn't normally when we're sick."

I'm trying hard to give him an out. Will he take it?

"Can I have a stuffed animal?"

I glance up at the giant net Ethan installed in the corner of Anna's room last year to try to contain all of her animals.

She has a ton of them, probably close to three dozen, stuffies she's been given for birthdays and holidays, ones she's begged for at the store. And yet, the only one she plays with is that purple bunny.

"Of course you can," I say, because right now I want him out of Anna's room. I don't know what it is, but something about him in here, by himself, without Anna around to play with him, feels wrong. "Grab one from up there," I say, pointing, but he's already picked up the bunny.

"This one."

"Not that one. You know as well as I do that that one is Anna's favorite and she'll freak out if anything happens to it. Choose another one and hop in bed, Micah. I'll be there with the thermometer to take your temperature in a minute."

With that, I sweep out of the room. I'm focused now and have something to do. Rather than mulling over what he was doing in Anna's room and the way he was holding her purple bunny to his chest like he didn't think he was going to be able to bear to part with it, I walk into the bathroom and rummage around in the drawers until I come up with the thermometer.

After pressing the button on the side once to turn it on and check the batteries, I walk into Micah's room.

He'd better be in here.

He is, thank goodness, a small brown bear in one hand. He's sitting on the edge of his bed and looks so small and sad that I almost feel bad for him.

But then I remember how creeped out he's been making me feel. How quickly he took to calling me "Mom." How alone I am in all of this.

"You ready, kiddo?" I ask, trying to sound cheerful. "Let's

see." With one hand I push his bangs back from his forehead —it's surprisingly cool, isn't it?—and with the other I press the thermometer to his skin.

Three seconds later there's a beep. I don't have to look at the screen to know that his temperature isn't high enough to trigger a warning from the thermometer. One beep is fine. Three, in quick succession, means he's got a fever.

"No fever," I say, stepping back from him and crossing my arms. "Do you feel like you're going to throw up? I was going to get you a trash can. Do you need it?"

"I'm feeling a lot better," he says, giving me a small smile. "I think that whatever it was must have passed."

"How fortuitous." My tone is sharp and I smile to take the edge off when I speak again. "I still think it's a good idea to rest for a bit. I'll keep your door open in case you call for me, but being up here in the quiet and dark will help you feel better faster."

"I don't want to be left alone." He stands up and I take a step back.

Man, he's tall. Sure, he's just a teenager, but I can't believe how tall he is. I have to look up at him and I feel silly that I never noticed that before.

"Well, I guess you can come lie down on the sofa," I say, because what other option do I have? If he doesn't want to be in his room, how in the world am I going to make him?

I don't think I can.

"That would be great, Mom, thank you. I'd... I'd rather be with you." He pushes past me and heads for the stairs.

I stand still, then press my hand to my pocket to feel for my phone.

It's only after a moment of panic shoots through me that I remember I left it in my purse. Downstairs.

"He wouldn't hurt you," I say, whispering the words to myself as I peek around the door into the hall. Micah's already going downstairs, and I'm sure he can't hear me from down there. "He's creepy, but he wouldn't hurt you."

Still, as I walk down the hall to the stairs, that thought doesn't give me much peace. All it does is raise another question in my mind.

But did he hurt his mom?

29

MICAH

I stretch out on the sofa, Anna's little bear tucked under my arm, and wait for Mom to come check on me. It's nice she agreed to let me come downstairs, since that's all I wanted—not to be alone.

School is hard. Even with the right clothes, even with parents who everyone knows and respects, it's hard. I've never been the popular kid and I didn't think that was going to happen overnight, but I still hoped kids would be nicer.

But they're not. At least Mom's nice. Dad's nice. Anna is nice.

I wanted to be home with Mom, to go with her to pick Anna up from preschool. Honestly, I don't think that's too much to ask, and when I told the nurse I didn't feel well, she got a little worried.

But only a little. So I ramped it up. Mentioned that I thought I was going to throw up.

That did the trick.

The officer the other night and the mean kids at school

could certainly make me feel like I might throw up, but that's not what happened.

I just wanted Mom. For the first time in my life I have a mother who wants to take care of me, who *will* take care of me and put me first, and I wanted to know what that felt like.

Some people might think it was a test, to see if she would do what I wanted her to, but that's not how I see it. Mom loves me, I know she does. She was so willing to open her house to me. But after the officer came by, it felt like things were different.

I guess I wanted to know that things were fine. I needed to make sure things hadn't gotten weird between us, that she was still happy having me here.

She's in the kitchen now; I can hear her moving around. She opens the fridge, a few cupboards.

I smile. Close my eyes. This is what I needed. Someone to take care of me the way my biological mother never did. Zoe will do it, though, I know she will.

I'm about to call out to her to ask her to come sit with me when I hear her cell ring. She swears, then there are heavy footsteps as she races across the kitchen to get it. She unzips her purse.

I hear it all perfectly.

"Hello?" Her voice is tight and she sounds worried. Over me? I don't want her to be that worried about me. I'll be fine.

"Yes, this is Zoe Steele. Thank you so much for calling me back." Her voice fades a little bit as she walks away. A moment ago I could hear her perfectly; she was close enough to the door leading into the family room. But now she's walking away.

I sit up, propping myself up on my elbow before giving up and looking over the back of the sofa.

"Yes, I drove by it too. They'd never heard of Rita."

My heart sinks. I want to hear more even though I'm sure I'm not going to like what she's saying, not if she's talking about *her*, and even though the right thing to do would be to lie back down and give Mom some privacy, I don't do that.

I'm practically crawling over the back of the sofa now. Originally, I'd wanted to be home so I didn't have to deal with other kids, so I could spend some time with Mom. Now, though, I'm grateful I'm here so I can tell what's going on.

"I can ask the school; surely they have the right address." Her voice fades. She's leaving the kitchen and walking out into the hall. Maybe she always walks and talks. Some people do that—they get on the phone and their feet start moving like they don't have any control over them.

Or maybe she doesn't want me to hear her.

This time, when she speaks, her voice is quiet enough— far away enough—that I can't make out the words. She sounds upset.

I hesitate.

Following her isn't the right thing to do. Nobody likes an eavesdropper, but if I stay here on the sofa then I'll never know what she was talking about.

My feet feel like they're on autopilot as I get up. Carefully, so I don't make any noise, I sneak out of the living room and into the kitchen. The dining table is in here and I pause by it, my ears pricked, my entire body on high alert.

Her voice floats towards me. If I get closer then maybe I'll be able to hear exactly what she's saying.

I certainly can't from where I am.

It's wrong, and I know it's wrong, but that doesn't stop me. I want to know what she's saying about me. At the door I pause, leaning up against the wall, my eyes closed so I can try to focus on her voice.

"Are you sure it's her?"

Silence. I'm barely breathing.

"He's actually home from school today," she tells me. "I can talk to him. You don't have to send an officer by."

Suddenly it's easier for me to understand what she's saying. I relax a little, grateful that I'm having an easier time hearing her and picking out the words. She must be talking louder, or clearer, or maybe I'm getting used to how quiet she is.

More footsteps.

"Of course I'll keep an eye on him. Thank you for letting me know. Hopefully it was all a misunderstanding. And I'll tell him about Rita."

She sounds like she's right next to me now.

Oh, my God, she sounds like she's right next to me now.

I leap away from the wall, my heart slamming hard in my chest. My feet feel like they're encased in concrete as I take one step back towards the living room, then another. She's still talking but I can't focus on any of her words. All I can hear is how much louder she's getting, how much closer she's gotten to me.

She's going to catch me standing here listening to her.

I spin around, determined to make a break for the living room, but my foot catches on a chair leg. For one moment I feel suspended in air, my arms pinwheeling around my head as I try to regain my balance, but then I'm tipping forward and there's no way to stop myself from falling.

My knees hit the floor first, the hard tile sending shock-waves up through my legs, but then I'm still tipping forward and I catch myself. The loud smack my palms make when they slam into the floor is met by silence.

I'm breathing hard, terrified Mom will have heard me.

Terrified of what she was talking about on the phone.

I'm still moving quickly as I try to stand so I can get out of the kitchen, but I risk a glance over my shoulder. Just in case. Because maybe she didn't hear me. Maybe I was loud, but not so loud she realized I was snooping.

Mom's standing there, the phone still pressed up to her ear. Her mouth is slightly open and her eyes are wide.

"Mom," I say, finally standing and turning to face her. My palms sting. My knees ache. I wouldn't be surprised if I lost some skin on them but I'm not going to look right now. "I'm sorry I was listening. That was wrong."

She doesn't respond.

I brush my hands on my pants. Man, they hurt.

"Officer, I'm going to have to call you back," she finally says.

My heart sinks.

A police officer? Again? My first thought is that she might have called the police because I came home from school when I wasn't actually sick and they were just now returning her call, but no. That's not something parents do, is it? If you miss a lot of school then the police will come to your home and ask what was going on. I know that much from reading books.

But parents don't call the police because you lied about not feeling great. Well, *lie* is a strong word. I stretched the truth, that's all.

But that means that they reached out to her.

That means they might have found my mom. Chills race

up my spine when I consider that possibility, that they found her.

That's absolutely the last thing I want to have happen.

30

ZOE

Micah watches me warily. He keeps his palms face up on his lap and I'm sure they hurt from him landing on them in the kitchen but you know what? I don't feel bad for him.

He was eavesdropping. He wasn't on the sofa, sick, where he was supposed to be. He got up and snuck towards me as soon as my back was turned. I didn't think he would do something like that.

But what do I honestly know about the boy?

Not enough, apparently.

I could push him and ask him what he was doing sneaking through the kitchen to listen to me, but I don't need to. I know the answer. He wanted to know who I was talking to. Maybe he knew it was the police, maybe he overheard that much of what was said.

And then I left the kitchen and he had no choice but to follow me if he wanted to keep up with what I was saying.

"Micah," I say, and he flinches. "I need you to look at me."

He does, and the expression on his face gives me pause. It's a mirror image of Ethan when he's upset. His jaw is set, tight. His eyes are a little narrow, like he's daring me to call him out on what he did. I watch as he purses his lips before relaxing them.

Even with his mouth relaxed, though, the rest of him is tight. Tense. His shoulders hunch up towards his ears and he's sitting straight, perfect posture, like he's waiting for the starting gun at a race.

"I drove by the address you gave me for your old house. Where you lived with your mother."

Nothing changes. There isn't any twitch of muscle on his face. His expression stays the same.

"The police went by there too, Micah. You never lived there."

He blinks. Slowly.

"Do you want to tell me your real address?"

"No."

That's exasperating. "Micah, Ethan and I want to help you, but you need to meet us halfway. You can't lie to us and expect us to accept it." I hear the frustration in my voice and I know it's not going to help anything with him but I can't seem to get it under control.

What the police have just told me...

"I'm sorry," he finally says. "I don't know why I lied."

Well, that's something.

"Micah, there's something else I need to tell you." I want to reach out for him, want to make sure he's getting the comfort he needs when I tell him what else the police said, but I can't seem to close the gap between us.

Any other child and I'd be right next to them, comforting them.

But I can't.

"The police... they found your mom."

"They found my mom?" His voice is flat.

Shouldn't he be hopeful? I know he likes living here—he's told me that over and over again—but shouldn't he be excited that they found Rita? Why isn't he?

"She's dead, Micah." My voice is quiet because I can't believe the words I'm saying.

"She's dead?" He parrots the words back to me, his eyes going wide. I'm desperate to read his mind, to know what's going on inside him as he sits so silently and looks at me.

I nod. My tongue is stuck to the roof of my mouth. Is how he's acting normal? Shouldn't he be crying? I know Rita wasn't the most maternal figure for Micah, but she was still his mother. I don't get why he isn't crying.

He's looking at me. Unblinking.

"I'm so sorry." *But who am I sorry for? Rita? Micah? Me?*

"How did they find her?"

My mind races. "Um, I think some of her friends hadn't seen her in a while and they called the police to let them know she was missing. Her friends told them where your mom liked to hang out. I guess they started looking there and expanded their search."

"Oh." He exhales, sits back. Still, his eyes never leave mine.

It's terrible, but I want to get more of a reaction out of him. I could tell him more, tell him how the police said they found her body in a ravine, how she'd been murdered, strangled, how bruised her face was. I could tell Micah that she'd been dumped, left there like a bag of trash. How it was pure luck that the police had expanded their search and someone happened to see a flash of color in the ravine.

But I'm not going to tell him that. He's in shock and telling him the gritty details will only make it worse. I'll keep it from him and I'll keep it from Ethan. They both knew Rita, and they don't need to be burdened with the mental image of how she died.

"Thank you." He blinks at me.

Thank you? "For what?"

"Letting me stay here. Taking me in." A strong exhale and he bends forward, resting his forehead in his hands.

We're silent, both of us unable to think of anything to say or do. I stare at him, unsure of what I should be doing now, unsure of how to handle this.

Why didn't he sound surprised? Why didn't he sound horrified?

Micah... accepted the information from me. I remember what it was like when I lost my mom in college, how I'd cried, how I'd sunk to the floor and sat there, dissolving into tears, how difficult it had been to try to function after that. Isn't that how most people react?

Even when your mom isn't kind, losing her feels like someone has jerked a rug out from under your feet. Like the world is tilted, leaning so far on its axis that the entire thing might fall over, like nothing in your life will ever be the same —or be okay—again.

And yet Micah barely bats an eye. It's like he had already prepared himself for this inevitability. Like he was aware that, at some point when she left him in the house, she wasn't going to return.

I don't know what it's like to have a mother continually walk out and then to not know if she's ever going to come back. I don't know how it feels to mourn a parent like that, to assume that they're dead. And maybe that's what he was doing—protecting himself and his heart by telling himself that she was dead each and every time she left him at home.

It makes sense if you think about it. If you prepare yourself for the worst, if you convince yourself that something terrible has already happened and there isn't anything you can do about it, then when the inevitable does occur, it's not as big a blow as it might have been.

He had to know that, at some point in his young life, his mother would walk out that door, put a needle in her arm and not come home.

But the officer didn't say she'd died of a drug overdose, did he?

And maybe Micah wasn't mentally prepared to hear that Rita was dead because he knew it was going to happen eventually.

Maybe he was mentally prepared for it because he already knew she was dead. And maybe he knew it because he's the one who killed her.

31

ZOE

In the end, I let Micah come with me to pick up Anna.

Not because I'm kind. Not because I'm worried about a tsunami of grief suddenly coming out of nowhere and taking him down, pain causing him to cry out and him possibly needing me. No, I bring him with me because I want to keep an eye on him.

I don't want him alone in the house. I don't like the idea of him in one of our bedrooms, poking around, maybe touching Anna's things, maybe in my room looking through my drawers.

The thought makes my skin crawl.

And he's not sick. I know he's not, even without checking his temperature again. Maybe he felt poorly at school not because kids are mean to him but because guilt will eat you up from the inside, no matter how much you think you can handle the thing you did.

And if he killed Rita...

I glance over at him, my hands tight on the steering wheel. What I need is to get rid of him so I can talk to Ethan, maybe call the police. Although, what would I say? That he's creepy? That I don't like having him in the house any longer? That even though I sat right there with an officer and promised that we'd take care of him I've changed my mind because I think he might have killed Rita?

"Hey, Mom? The line's moving." Micah reaches over and lightly touches my arm, his other hand pointing through the windshield.

I gasp and jerk my arm away from him, then look ahead of us, guilt washing over me. "Thanks," I manage, pressing down on the gas to close the gap between me and the car ahead of me. Normally I'm in the front of the line, waiting on Anna so she doesn't feel like she has to wait on me. But right now I'm towards the back of the line.

Even though I couldn't wait to get out of the house and come get my girl, I wasn't sure that bringing Micah was the right thing.

But I didn't have any other choice. He had to come with me, and me taking so long to accept that is the reason I'm later than normal to get my little girl.

We pull up in front of the school and I'm embarrassed at the small crowd of kids left. Anna is officially one of the last kids to be picked up, but when I finally spot her standing with a friend, she doesn't seem bothered. Her ponytail, which I'd worked hard to get tight right on the back of her head, is sagging. She has her little owl backpack slung over one arm and there's a bit of blue paint on her shirt that wasn't there when she left the house this morning.

Looking at her makes my heart swell. No matter what I'm going through with Micah right now, I know things are going to work out in the end, and that's because I have Anna. She's perfect. She's delightful and wonderful and...

And I have to keep her safe.

"There she is!" Micah rolls down the window and waves out of it. "Hi, Anna! I came to pick you up today!"

She turns, a question on her face, but then she sees Micah and she grins, waving back. "My brudder!" Such a cute little way she says it, and I know I should be grateful that she has someone in her life she's so excited about seeing, but the way she runs at the car, her backpack bouncing, makes my heart drop.

Mrs. Denise is right behind her and opens the door, reaching out to help her into the car, but Anna clambers in without waiting for assistance.

"Micah was sick and he came home from school early," I tell her, wanting to beat him to the punch. "I don't think he's super contagious, but I want you to keep your distance a little, in case he is. You need to buckle up, unbuckle, all of that stuff all on your own. And instead of you two playing together this afternoon, Micah's probably going to read in his room. Or on the sofa."

"You're sick?" Anna leans forward, her little face right between ours. "How sick?"

"I feel fine," he says, but I cut him off from saying anything else.

"Anna, sit. Buckle in. We gotta move so other kids can go home." I'm gripping the steering wheel so tightly I feel like my hands are going to cramp. I want to scream at her to hurry up, to move faster, but she takes her time, settling back in her car seat, still talking to Micah about how he feels.

As soon as I hear the little click from her seatbelt, I hit the gas, driving away from the preschool. Now I have Anna, and that's good because I can keep an eye on her. I can keep her and Micah apart so nothing bad happens to her.

I run through the mental list of things I need to do today.

Keep the two of them separate.

Make dinner.

Do laundry.

Get them in bed so Ethan and I can talk.

My stomach twists when I think about how that conversation is going to go. What will Ethan say when I tell him that not only is Rita dead, but that I think Micah may have had something to do with it? That his son has been creeping me out for a while now but I haven't told him because I couldn't find the time?

And that I felt bad for him?

Well, I don't feel bad now. Glancing over, I'm not surprised to see Micah has turned around in his seat. He's grinning at Anna, who's chattering a mile a minute about her day and how much fun she had at preschool.

I should be thrilled that Anna is so happy, that she loves talking to Micah, that she feels a connection with him like this. But I'm not.

"Hey, Micah." My voice comes out sharper than I mean it to. "You need to turn around, got it? If your stomach wasn't feeling good earlier today and you're facing backwards, you might get sick. That's the last thing we want."

He turns around slowly, pausing to look at me.

"Thank you." I swallow hard, glancing at him before looking back at the road ahead of us. "I think looking ahead is best. It's been a long day."

Micah doesn't answer. He yanks down the rearview mirror and angles it so he can see Anna. "Hey, Anna Banana," he says, lifting his hand and wiggling his fingers to get her attention. "Guess what?"

She loves guessing games. "What?"

"The police called. They found my real mom and she's dead. I'm staying with you now."

Anna laughs. She claps her hands together.

Horrified, I glance over at Micah. He's still looking at her in the mirror, a grin slashed across his face. I feel like I'm going to throw up and I force myself to look away from him, to keep my eyes on the road.

I have to talk to Ethan.

Originally I wanted to do right by Micah but Anna's the only thing that matters now.

Anna stares at me from the kitchen table, her eyebrows furrowed, her mouth pressed into a thin line.

I know she's not pleased with me for keeping her here in the kitchen with me and not allowing her to go play with Micah, but I want to keep the two of them apart as much as possible.

Him coming home from school because he told the nurse he was sick makes that easier for me. If he hadn't come home early from school then I'd have to come up with a reason to keep the two of them apart. I don't want him near Anna right now, not until I talk to Ethan. Not until I tell him what my worries are.

"You know, if you don't eat your pizza, you're going to be hungry in bed," I say, pulling out a chair to sit down across from her. "And there won't be anything else for you to eat before breakfast tomorrow."

"I want brudder." She crosses her arms and stares at me, giving me time to look down at her plate to try to judge how much she's had to eat. Almost a whole slice. Not enough, but I don't feel like fighting with her. Right now, all I want is to get the two of them in bed and talk to Ethan.

I glance at my wrist. He should be home anytime now. Sure, sometimes patients need extra care and he ends up staying later, but come on. The one night I need him here more than anything else, and he's not rushing home as soon as possible to get to me?

I feel like I'm coming out of my skin. Ethan isn't to blame for this, not unless I want to blame him for being in a relationship with someone way before I knew him, which isn't fair. I have to hold it together here a little bit longer and then it will all be over.

What the end result will be, I don't know. I can't think about that right now.

"Okay then," I finally say, snapping back to attention. "You don't want to eat more, Anna? You'll be hungry, but you'll survive. Let's head upstairs and put on your pjs."

Her mouth drops open. "But dessert! And I want to see Daddy!"

"Daddy will be here when he gets here," I tell her, hurrying around the table before she can try to make a break for it. "You and I are going to go upstairs and get you tucked in. Then Micah is going to bed. Tomorrow everyone will feel better and you can sleep in, because it's Saturday. How does that sound?"

She's about to open her mouth to argue with me, I can tell. I see that she's gearing up for a royal battle, not only in the way she throws her head back to look at me, but in how she clenches her fists at her sides, but before she can make a sound, Micah speaks.

He's right behind me. I was so focused on my daughter that I never heard him sneak up.

"I can take her and put her to bed, Mom. I know she can be grumpy when she doesn't want to go."

When I turn to look at him, he smiles at me, then reaches for Anna.

The little traitor practically lunges out of her chair to get to him.

"No, you don't have to." I try to step in between them, but kids are fast when they want something, and somehow even faster when the thing that they want is something you don't want them to have. "Seriously, Micah, you've been sick."

"I feel fine." There's an edge to his voice I don't like.

Rather than fighting with him, I step back, my arms hanging uselessly at my sides. I could try to get involved, but she's taking his hand like she couldn't be happier. In the time it takes me to blink, he has her on his hip and is walking around the table.

I look at his hands, how big they are as he holds her, how confidently he carries her. *He's strong*, I realize with a start. Stronger than I thought a young teenage boy would be.

"I'll come with you," I say, because now I'm desperate not to let the two of them out of my sight. He might have won this one, might get to put her to bed, but I'm going to be right there with them. I want to make sure he doesn't...

What? Hurt her? He loves her.

Just like he loved his mom?

"I've got it," Micah tells me.

But I stay on his heels all the way up the stairs. I have a sudden, terrible, all-consuming mental image of him tripping on the stairs and falling backwards, Anna flying out of his arms.

"Let me brush her teeth," I start to say.

Anna cuts me off. "Brudder will do it. I want Micah."

It's the first time I've heard her call him by his name and I stop in my tracks, breathing hard, watching as he snuggles her close. When he turns to look at me, there's a triumphant expression on his face. I stand, horrified, watching as he takes her into the bathroom.

But I'm not letting him go in there with her alone. A moment later I'm in the door, watching, not looking away from them as he carefully brushes her teeth, tells her to wash her face. She brushes her hair while he watches, then he helps her down from the counter and they brush past me to go to her room.

"I can handle this," he tells me. "Why don't you trust me, Mom?"

"I want to be there for you," I lie. "You weren't feeling good, Micah."

"You don't think I can handle helping Anna get ready for bed." He stares at me like he's trying to think something through. "You don't want her to be alone with me, but you were fine with it before. You were fine with us playing together and now you don't want that. Why not, Mom?"

"Because you're sick." My words sound false, even to my ears, and I can only imagine how obvious it is that I'm lying. He has to be able to see right through me.

Sure enough, he scoffs, turning away from me and shaking his head. "I thought you were happy to have me here," he mutters, his voice low and dark. He stares down the hall to Anna's room.

My daughter has disappeared in there to put on her pajamas. I need to help her—she always gets her head stuck in her shirt and will scream until she's free—but I don't want to look away from Micah.

I'm suddenly very aware of how close I'm standing to the top of the stairs. Of how tall Micah is. Of how close he's standing to me. Of how easy it would be for him to push me.

Rita was found dead in a ravine.

"We are happy to have you here," I say, trying my best to fix this, to smooth things over.

Micah shakes his head so violently his hair flops back and forth on his forehead. "No, you're not. You were, but you're not. I don't get it, but you're like every other adult. I thought you were different." His hands are fists. Tight. He stares at me, his face drawn.

I don't like the way his eyes dart back and forth between mine like he's trying to tell if I'm lying about something.

I don't like any of this.

"I like having you here," I say. "You're sick. When we don't feel good, things can feel out of our control." That's my story and I'm sticking to it. I'm never going to admit to him that I don't want him near Anna. I'll lie about that until I die if that's what it takes.

"Sick. Right." He taps the side of his head and my stomach sinks. "That's what you want to say to me so you don't have to tell me the truth. That you don't like me like you thought you would." He looks so sad that I feel my heart breaking. "I'm going to bed." He brushes past me to go to his room, lightly brushing against me with his shoulder.

For a moment, I keep my balance, then I feel like I'm falling, the ground rising up to meet me, only the ground is the first floor of the house and I have an entire set of stairs to slam down first and...

No. Stop. He barely touched me with his shoulder. Even

if he'd knocked right into me, I'm not going anywhere. I watch as he slams his door. I listen to the sound of him locking it.

Then I go to Anna's room. I haven't had her baby monitor on in more than a year but I pull it out from her closet and plug it in right by her bed, turning it on and clipping the receiver onto my waistband. I have to leave the two of them up here so I can talk to Ethan, but there's no way I'm going to let Micah get to my daughter.

I don't know what to do now, but Ethan will help me figure it out. He always does.

Yes, we invited Micah in. Of course, that was the right thing to do. But now I don't think it is. I made a mistake. I'm going to tell Ethan everything, and then I'm going to fix this.

I don't have a choice.

33

MICAH

I lay on my bed in my jeans, my shoes still on my feet, but even though I'm uncomfortable, I don't move to take them off. I have pajamas Mom bought me, comfortable ones that I know would feel better on my body and would help me sleep better than my clothes will, but I don't want to be comfortable.

I don't deserve it.

My mind races as I try to think about what I did wrong. What Mom found out that would turn her against me. She was the one here who opened her arms to me, who seemed to want me to live with her family, and now all of that changed, and I don't know what happened.

I really don't.

I thought I was being a good brother, a good son. I thought I was fitting in. I thought seeing the two of us in a picture together would make it more real for me, would help me see Zoe as my mom, and it worked.

And now she doesn't want me.

Maybe she hated the picture. Maybe she realized the

responsibility she took on by letting me move into her house.

I guess it was a terrible idea, even though it seemed like a good one at the time.

Heat rushes through my body and I sit up, yanking my sneakers off and throwing them at the wall. They hit with loud slams then fall to the ground. My heart pounds and I gasp for air, twisting my fingers in my sheets as I try to calm down.

But it's almost impossible.

If they hadn't ever found my biological mom then maybe things would be better. Maybe that's the problem, that they found her and now Zoe feels bad about being my mom. She's been reminded that I already had one, even though she was pretty terrible.

But I don't think that's it. There's more to it.

She loved me and now she's pulling back. It's like she doesn't love me anymore.

And that fact makes me so angry I could scream.

34

ZOE

I'm waiting with a glass of wine by the garage door when Ethan comes home. Even though something strong would have definitely taken the edge off the evening, I haven't wanted to drink. I need him to see that I'm completely in control, that I haven't had anything that would affect how I'm handling what's going on.

A glass of wine would certainly dull the edge of how upset I'm feeling, but it wouldn't be good in the long run. This is for Ethan, to help him stay calm while we talk.

"What a surprise." Ethan takes the wine from me and then kisses me, his hand spread wide on the small of my back.

I pull away from him, suddenly thinking about Micah's hands, how big they are, how easy it would be for him to hurt someone with them. He has his father's hands, only Ethan uses his for healing. Did Micah use his to kill his mom?

"I need to talk to you," I say, but he's already walked past me into the kitchen.

"Where are the kids?"

"In bed." I pause, then reach for him to get his attention. "Ethan, hey. Come on, into the living room. There are some things we need to talk about."

"Yeah, sorry about that earlier," he says, leading the way to his favorite sofa. He sits and takes a sip of wine. "I know you were trying to get in touch with me but I had so many patients to operate on this morning that calling you back when you had to go wasn't on my to-do list. What's going on? And why are the kids in bed so early?"

"Anna was exhausted," I lie, "and I had to pick Micah up from school early because he was sick. But I want to talk to you—"

"He's sick?" Ethan leans forward, obviously concerned. "What's wrong with him?"

"Honestly, I don't know. He told the nurse he felt ill and that he might throw up, but he's been fine since I got him home. I don't think he wanted to be at school, if I'm being honest with you."

Ethan nods. Takes another sip. "He's going through a rough time. I'm glad we can be there to help him. And, you know, everyone understands."

"What?" I'm so caught up on thinking about Micah lying that I don't immediately follow his line of thinking.

"About him. I was in college. You were right, nobody seems to be bothered by the fact that I had a child I didn't know about. If anything, they all blame Rita for keeping him from me."

"Oh, yeah, I figured that would happen. But listen, Ethan, I need to talk to you about Micah."

"I hate to use his problems as a boost for me, but that's what's happening." Ethan grins at me, happy about how his life is going, but then catches the dark expression on my face. "I'm sorry, Zoe, I'm dominating the conversation. What's happening?"

For a moment I consider the possibility that maybe I'm insane, that things aren't nearly as bad as I think they are, that I'm letting my imagination run away from me. Maybe I've been taking things too seriously rather than letting them roll off my back, but I know that's not true.

"I'm worried about Micah," I say, keeping my voice soft. Before I continue I glance over my shoulder to make sure he hasn't suddenly appeared. "He's been doing some things that are creepy."

"Creepy." Ethan sits up straighter. "How so?"

"Remember how you discovered that the picture of me from the fridge was missing?" When my husband nods, I continue. "That's because Micah cut my head off and glued it on Rita's body."

He blinks at me.

"He had a photo of him and Rita," I say, desperate for Ethan to understand. "And he cut my head off and glued it on Rita's body so it's like the two of us are holding hands. And then he lied to me about his address. I told you about that."

He frowns. "You don't think that's because he's a kid who probably wasn't ever taught his address? I know how you work with Anna to make sure she knows where she lives and that I work at the hospital, but you know as well as I do that Rita probably never did any of that. I bet she was too busy doing drugs to teach him anything like that."

I wave my hand in the air. "But there's more." I stand up, suddenly overcome by the desire to move around. I feel like

I'm coming out of my skin and the way Ethan is watching me, so calm, so in control, it's maddening.

"She's dead," I say, pointing at him to ensure I have his attention. I need to tell him about the internet searches on Micah's laptop, but right now that feels more incriminating to me than him. "Rita. I talked to the police."

"Oh, my God." Ethan sags back into the sofa. "She's dead? What happened?"

I shrug. This isn't going the way I thought it would. He seems to have an answer for everything I'm saying and I'm honestly starting to feel a little stupid.

"They found her dead; I don't know more than that. They said she'd been attacked, so it's a murder. But I don't know what they're going to do now. Look for who killed her, I guess."

"Holy shit. Did you tell Micah?"

"Of course I did, yeah."

"And how did he take it?"

How do I tell Ethan that Micah didn't seem bothered by the fact his mother was found dead? He didn't seem to care, no matter how you try to spin it.

"He was fine," I say, choosing my words carefully. "No, actually, Ethan, that's not fair. I don't think it bothered him."

He's silent for a moment. "I can't imagine what he's going through. What he's *gone* through. If I'd known about him, if I'd been there, none of this might have happened." He exhales hard and closes his eyes.

"Hey, no." I sit next to him, reaching over and wrapping my arms around his torso. "This is not your fault, Ethan. You didn't know about Micah, but that's on Rita, not you. She was into some bad things. Drugs. Drinking. Who knows who she was hanging out with? You couldn't have ever predicted this would happen."

"I feel so terrible for him," Ethan tells me, then turns to me, cupping my cheek with his free hand. He sighs. "Thank you."

I'm surprised. "For what?"

"Telling me we needed to take care of him. I was so selfish to even think about turning him away. But he needs us. He needs you."

"Ethan, there's something else." It's now or never and even though I don't want to tell him what I did, I don't think I have much of an option any longer. "I snooped through his laptop."

"You what?" His hand falls from my cheek. I want it back, desperately want to feel his skin on mine, but he's staring at me like he doesn't know who I am.

"After I went to his house and discovered he'd never lived there. I got scared, Ethan, that maybe you'd been right and I'd pushed you to let him in when we didn't know anything about him. I looked on his computer and I know I shouldn't have, but you need to know what I found."

Silence.

"He'd been looking us up," I tell him, the words spilling out of me now. There's no taking them back, no undoing what I'm telling him. "Saving pictures of me. He's known about us for a while."

I might have made a huge mistake in coming clean to my husband, but I had to do it. He needs to know what I do, so we can decide what to do next. So we can decide how we're going to handle this. Together as a team. No matter what happens, I know one thing. We'll keep Anna safe.

"Zoe." He exhales. Drains his wine. When he shifts

forward to put the empty glass on the coffee table, I have to move away from him to give him room.

"I didn't mean to! It's not like I planned on doing it, but then things were getting so weird and I didn't know what to do."

"You shouldn't have done that."

"I know. It was wrong, but don't you see, Ethan? I learned things that we wouldn't have otherwise known! What if we never knew about him looking us up? About him saving pictures of me? It's weird. Creepy. I don't like it." I shiver, and even though I'm sure it looks fake, like I'm trying to be dramatic, I'm not.

I swear I'm not.

It's just that thinking about all of this, considering what it might mean for our family and the implications of him stalking me, makes me sick.

"He's a kid, Zoe. With a crappy home life."

"He was stalking me."

Ethan sighs and rolls his head back, his eyes closed. He was so calm when he got home, so relaxed, and I know I'm the reason he's under so much stress right now, but I don't care. All I did was bring a problem to his attention. It was the right thing to do, no matter what happens next.

"Listen, honey, I can't even begin to imagine what it was like growing up as Micah. Rita was... well, she was fun. But she wasn't stable and she obviously went off the deep end after she had him. I'm sorry I wasn't there for him to keep him safe when he was a little kid. But I'm there now."

"Ethan, listen to me." I'm doing my best to keep my voice even and calm. Right now, though, I want to scream. "I need you to listen to me. I think he killed his mother."

Ethan stands, the movement explosive, and I rock back

from him. "Zoe, that is my son." He's whisper-yelling and stabs his finger up to the ceiling. "My son. I don't know what terrible things he's lived through."

"I know, but—"

"And I'm sorry that you're creeped out, but maybe instead of jumping to that conclusion, you consider the fact that he might be troubled. He needs therapy. He needs, more than someone judging him and thinking he's a terrible person, for someone to love him. To counsel him."

I'm being admonished. This is what it must feel like at the hospital when Ethan is upset about something and he blows up at a nurse. I want to remind him that I'm his *wife*, not a nurse, that he can't talk to me like this, but instead I sit in silence.

"You welcomed him in because it was the right thing to do." Ethan frowns at me. "Remember? And I wasn't totally on board but I am now because that boy is my son. You were right then, and I was wrong. You told me he could be with us, and now he's here. We're going to protect him. I need your help with that. We can get him a therapist, don't you think? Next week."

I nod but the movement is mechanical. My hand reaches to my side and I lightly touch the baby monitor receiver, just to make sure it's still there.

Ethan can protect Micah all he wants. The only child I'm worried about protecting right now is Anna.

35

ZOE

Saturday March 18

I wake early in the morning, the sound of an obnoxious wren right outside my window making me roll out of bed. It's not even spring yet, the days are still too chilly for planting, the nights cold enough to bring frost, but this stupid bird obviously hasn't gotten the memo and is busy screaming into the sky.

"Shut up, bird," I whisper, without thinking, then freeze. Ethan's probably still asleep. He was up a long time last night and even though the phone never rang while we were in bed, I'm pretty sure I felt him tossing and turning last night as much as I was.

I slip out from the covers and slowly turn back, grabbing my phone and tapping the screen to illuminate it as I pick up the baby monitor receiver. Thank goodness there wasn't a sound out of this all night, which tells me Anna never made a peep. Still, I did put her to bed early last night, so I have no doubt she'll be up sooner rather than later.

Might as well get downstairs and start making breakfast.

I tiptoe across the bedroom and into the bathroom where I take a quick shower. After my morning routine, I head downstairs, careful to close the bedroom door all the way behind me. The last thing I want is to wake Ethan and have him be in a mood.

Our conversation last night did not go how I thought it would. Honestly, I'd assumed he'd be right there with me, taking my side, backing me up. But as soon as a I painted Micah in a less than flattering light, Ethan had freaked out. It was almost funny considering how he hadn't particularly wanted the boy to live with us in the first place.

Downstairs I turn on the coffeepot and light a candle. Weak light streams in through the kitchen windows so I turn on the light above the window, brightening up the room enough to allow me to see. My stomach rumbles and I walk to the fridge, digging deep in it to see what I'm going to make for breakfast.

Pancakes. Apple slices, because the apples I bought two weeks ago are starting to look a little rough. Scrambled eggs with... I open the cheese drawer. Feta, I guess. We also have milk and juice and I put those on the table before looking back in the fridge for anything else we might need.

Nope, looks like that's it. Closing the door, I turn, then jump.

Someone's standing in the doorway.

"Hi, Mom." Micah sounds hesitant, like he's not sure if he's welcome. He takes a step into the kitchen, then another, then pulls out a chair and sits at the table. "I heard you come downstairs and thought I'd join you. I couldn't sleep."

"Hi." I grab four glasses from the cupboard. "Here, why don't you get yourself something to drink?"

He reaches out for the glass but I put it down on the table instead of handing it to him. It's crappy, and I know that, but I don't want our fingers to touch.

"Do you want help making breakfast? I can crack the eggs."

"No, I've got it." My back is to him as I reach for the box of pancake mix in a high cupboard. My fingers brush the box and I push it back, sliding it a little farther out of reach. "Come on," I mutter under my breath.

"Need help with that? I can reach it easier than you can." Micah's by my side before I can stop him, his hand brushing past mine, his hip knocking into mine. I have the box. It's barely in my fingers, but I'm still holding onto it. But then his elbow is in the way and it hits me.

I take a step back, losing my balance, and the box is above my head until it isn't. I watch, in horror, as the box tips, then falls, Micah trying to grab it out of the air, me standing there unable to do anything but stare.

It slams into the ground, a puff of white pancake mix like a nuclear cloud above it before settling on everything in the kitchen.

Me. Micah. The floor. The counter. It reaches to the table and the closest chair now has a fine layer of pancake mix like dust on the seat and legs.

"Oh, I'm sorry." Micah takes a step back from me, his eyes wide and locked on mine, his hand reaching up to cover his mouth. "Mom, I'm so sorry."

"Don't call me that." I snap the words before I even realize they were on my mind to say. "Stop stepping in it. You're making it worse."

"I said I'm sorry." Micah's voice is quieter now but his eyes, if anything, have gotten wider. He's staring at me like he's never seen me before. "I didn't mean to upset you."

I have no idea if he's referencing upsetting me by calling me Mom or spilling the pancake mix everywhere but I'm not in the mood to ask him. Ethan thinks he needs a shrink to psychoanalyze him and make him feel better about his childhood, but I can't do that for him.

"Micah... leave the kitchen. I'll clean it all up and make breakfast. It's easier that way." I'm still snapping at him and I know I need to stop but I can't make myself. "You can go relax before breakfast."

He doesn't move. "But I wanted to spend time with you."

I take a deep breath, hold the air in my lungs for as long as I can, then slowly exhale. The thought of Micah spending time with me right now while I'm trying to make breakfast— while I'm trying to do *anything*, really—is enough to make me scream.

"This is a pretty big mess, Micah," I say, making sure my tone is even. "I'm sorry I snapped at you, but honestly, the best thing is for you to leave so I can clean this up. I'll be able to get it swept up and still get breakfast going before Ethan and Anna are awake."

"I can get her for you." He's bouncing on the balls of his feet, obviously eager to please. "Let me get her."

"No!" The word is so loud, so demanding, that both of us freeze. "No," I say, slower and softer this time. "Thank you. But I have her monitor here and I'll know if she needs me. She wants me in the morning."

He mumbles something under his breath but turns away from me, walking carefully out of the kitchen into the living room.

I stand completely still watching him go.

Keep going. Don't stop. Keep going.

The light in the other room clicks on. He walks over to Ethan's favorite sofa and stretches out on it.

Thank God.

It's time for me to sweep this up. I have purpose now and I move quickly, grabbing the broom from where we keep it stashed by the refrigerator. It won't take me too long to clean this all up, but I'm much happier doing it on my own.

I didn't want Micah hovering. Or trying to help. I don't want him anywhere near me, if I'm being honest. I need a break from him, need some space.

And the thought of him going upstairs to get Anna? My skin crawls.

No, I don't know what I'm going to do about Micah. But Ethan isn't worried about him like I am.

That means I have only one choice.

I think he killed his mother. If I'm going to get him out of my house, I have to prove it.

36

ZOE

Micah stays in the living room while I put together breakfast, thank goodness. I don't think I could have handled him coming back in, asking to help once again. If anything, I might have snapped at him and told him that I know what really happened to his mother.

And that wouldn't have been good. My mind races as I finish plating the pancakes and put the syrup on the table. What I don't understand is why Ethan is suddenly so calm about Micah being here. I know I was the one who originally wanted to support the boy, who wanted to open our home to him.

But he changed his mind, didn't he? He wasn't totally on board at first, but he is now, and I can't help but wonder what it was that made him change. It has to be work, it has to be the fact that now people know about Micah and they support him—and me—for allowing the boy to live here.

It's the only difference I can think of.

Ethan's reputation has always been incredibly important

to him. He's always been careful about making sure that everything we do, everything we put on social media, all of our interactions outside of the home make us look the best we can. I've thought it was silly, over the years.

I mean, come on. People argue. Couples fight, but that doesn't mean they don't love each other. It doesn't mean they're going to get a divorce. I still remember how surprised I was the time Ethan set me down after we were out to dinner together and I'd gotten mad at him in the restaurant.

What's funny is that I don't remember why I was upset with him in the first place. All I know is that something he said made me angry and I argued with him. The waiter walked by and there was a chance the man heard us going at it, but who cares?

Ethan did, apparently. We got home, me buzzing a little from the wine I'd had at dinner, completely unaware that we hadn't smoothed things over the way I thought we had. Ethan was the opposite, stiff and quiet, obviously upset, but I wasn't planning on letting that ruin my evening. There's nothing worse than having a nice little buzz and someone ruining it because they're not in a great mood.

But that's what happened. Even though it's been years since that happened, I can still remember how he asked me to come sit next to him on that stupid leather sofa of his. I remember how he put his hand on my knee, how I thought the evening was about to end up with us in bed together.

"Zoe," he'd told me, his eyes locked on mine, his face serious. "Don't argue with me out in public. People need to think that we never fight, that we're always on the same page. It's important for my career. Promise me you won't make people ever think that I'm less than perfect again."

I'd been surprised, but I promised. And, since then, I've done everything in my power to make him look his best.

Until I put my foot down and invited Micah into our home. But that worked out for him, didn't it? Ethan took my advice and told Bonnie at work about how we'd opened our home to the poor boy and now everyone at the hospital knew how amazing my husband was.

I'm so lost in thought, remembering the surprise I'd felt when Ethan told me never to argue with him in public again, that I don't realize he's entered the kitchen. Anna's on his hip, a huge grin on her face, and I take her, snuggling her against me.

"My little girl," I say, giving her a kiss. "Did you sleep well? You two were so quiet that I never heard you on your monitor." She's still warm from bed and she presses her face into my neck, her arms around my neck.

"Where's brudder?" Her little voice is soft, so perfect.

I hate that she doesn't give me a chance to respond before she squirms from my grasp and races out of the kitchen. I don't want her to go but before I can follow her, before I can scoop her back up, my husband speaks and I turn to him.

"Where is Micah?" Ethan sounds concerned but he visibly relaxes when I jut my thumb over my shoulder at the living room. "Good. Are you feeling better about last night?"

"Everything is fine." I smile at my husband, then lean in and give him a kiss. "I'm sure you're right; it's all a misunderstanding. But I do think we need to hire a therapist. It's only fair that we get him the help he needs. I can take care of his body and feed him and make sure he rests, but his mental health needs help too."

Ethan sighs. Runs a hand through his hair. When he

does speak, it's over his shoulder, and he's already halfway to the coffee pot. "I'll handle it. There's already so much on your plate that it doesn't seem fair to ask you to do more."

"Thank you." I'm surprised by that but do my best to keep the shock out of my voice. Ethan doesn't like handling *household problems.* He'd much rather I be the one to take care of anything related to our kid. *Kids.*

"No problem." He takes a sip of his coffee. "Hey, kids, come on in here. Your mom has been up making a delicious breakfast and we're gonna start without you!"

Micah appears in the doorway almost instantly, almost like he was waiting for an invitation. He's grinning and smiles at Ethan before skirting around me to his chair. Anna's there a moment later, the teddy bear Micah borrowed from her room yesterday clutched in her hand.

I watch the two of them as they pull out their chairs. Anna's already reaching for a pancake but Ethan stops her, his movements gentle, a smile on his face. He turns to me and gestures to the table.

"You coming, honey? This looks delicious and we all know the chef has to have first bite."

"Right." I rub my hands together. Suddenly, I'm so cold. It's not chilly in the kitchen, not by a long shot, but I feel cold, like the chill is internal. "I'm glad you guys are hungry."

Ethan is still smiling at me. Anna has managed to wrangle a pancake from the serving plate and has it on her plate, her eyes wide as she takes in the crisp edges, the golden brown color.

But then I look at Micah. He's staring at me, his face expressionless. At the last moment he attempts to arrange his face into a smile, but I turn away from him, not wanting to see.

He can smile at people all he wants. I shined him up, bought him new clothes, and I'm showing him how to be the type of person others will respect. But that's all on the outside.

I've seen glimpses of who he really is. Maybe Ethan doesn't want to believe me, doesn't want to see Micah for who he is on the inside because he's his son.

But I've seen the truth. Micah's living in our house because I invited him in. But I'm going to protect my family from him.

I'm going to make sure he can't tear us apart.

37

ZOE

After breakfast we all split up. Ethan goes outside to putter and Anna and Micah leave me in the kitchen to pick up. Normally I'd want help, want someone there to wash dishes or at least put them in the dishwasher, but I don't mind the alone time right now.

It gives me a chance to think.

I clean up quickly, knowing that even though I can hear the kids playing in the living room, they may decide to move to a new location at any moment. Right now, I want nothing more than to keep an eye on them, to make sure Micah doesn't do or say anything to Anna that will upset her.

Before leaving the kitchen, I hang the towel on the oven door, then step back and look around. Perfectly clean. Perfectly neat. Everything is ready for when I need to make lunch, which will happen a lot sooner than you'd think.

I'm always amazed at how quickly each meal follows the one before it. It's a never-ending cycle, me in the kitchen cooking, cleaning, cooking, cleaning, like a treadmill I can't get off.

But that's life. It's what I signed up for when I got pregnant with Anna and quit my job at the hospital. It was the right thing for Ethan, for us, and I was more than willing to change my plans to accommodate our growing family. I don't think there are a lot of women who would be willing to do what I did, to change their life so completely, but it made sense for us. That's how much I love Ethan. That's how much I love Anna.

I'm about to walk into the living room to check on the kids when Anna comes running through the door. She slams into my legs, her little arms wrapping around me, and I drop to my knees, wanting to simultaneously push her away so I can get a better look at her and pull her close so I can hold her and never let her go.

"Anna! Are you okay?" I grip her shoulders, feeling how skinny she is.

"It hurst," she moans in response. Movement out of the corner of my eye catches my attention before I can respond, and I look up. It's Micah, standing in the doorway, his eyes wide.

"What did you do?" Even I hear the venom in my voice. It's thick, dripping from the four words, and Micah takes a step back, holding up one hand between us like that would ever be enough to stop me from getting to him if he hurt my little girl.

"We were playing and she jammed her finger against the back of the sofa." The hand is still up. It wavers between us but he never looks away from my face. "She ran in here before I could get a good look at it to make sure she wasn't badly hurt."

"How did she jam it?" I ask, even though what I want to say is *how did you hurt her*?

He shrugs. "We were playing with the bear and she lunged for it. She missed and jammed her thumb."

I stare at him for another moment, the scene of what happened playing out in my mind. I can see him taunting her, holding the bear above his head so she had to reach for it, making it impossible for her to get her teddy bear back without stretching, without putting herself in a precarious position, until she fell and landed on her thumb.

It's probably broken. Probably snapped to the side. He has to know how upset I'm going to be. That's why he looks concerned, not because he's worried about her being hurt, but because he's worried about what I'm going to do to him.

But then I look down at Anna. She has her thumb held out, her eyes wide with tears.

And her thumb looks fine. If I didn't know any better, if he hadn't told me she'd hurt it, I'd never know anything was going on.

"Anna," I say, my words measured and careful, "did Micah hurt your thumb?"

"No! I didn't!" He takes a step into the kitchen but freezes when I look up at him.

"Anna, what happened?"

"No," she sniffles, still staring at her thumb. "I fell. Brudder didn't do anything."

"I told you." Micah spits the words at me. They're half-under his breath, but still loud enough for me to hear them.

Rather than looking up at him, though, rather than giving him the attention I'm sure he wants right now, I ignore him.

"Are you okay, baby?" I ask, brushing some of Anna's hair back from her forehead. "Do you want an ice pack?"

"No." Now she whips her thumb away from me. "I want to play."

"But honey, if your thumb is hurt then I think you need to let me ice it. It will feel better in the long run and I can keep it from bruising and swelling."

"Mom." Anna grabs both of my cheeks and stares into my eyes. "I want to play."

Then she's gone, running towards Micah. I look up in time to watch as she grabs his hand with her good hand, laughter pouring out of her. She's trying to drag him back into the living room where they were playing before, but he's not moving. He's standing completely still.

I force myself to look up at him, to drag my eyes away from my little girl. Micah's staring right at me. His face is so closed off I can't even begin to imagine what he's thinking, but I have a feeling it's nothing good.

We stay like that for what feels like minutes but has to only be seconds. Anna pulling on his hand, desperate to take him back into the living room so the two of them can play together. Me staring at Micah, trying my hardest to read his mind, to tell what he's thinking before he allows Anna to drag him out of the room.

And Micah. Staring at me. Watching me.

Measuring me.

38

MICAH

Anna presses the teddy bear into my hand but I shake my head before she can speak.

"Anna, I don't want you to get hurt again." My voice is low because I don't want anyone else to hear what I'm saying to her. "I'm serious. Why don't we do a puzzle or something?"

She frowns, but only for a moment, then breaks into a grin. "Deal. You wait here."

I watch as she slips from the sofa and runs to the far side of the room where she has a game closet. The door sticks a bit but she yanks on it, putting all of her weight into it, and it opens with a creak.

I can't help but smile. She's just so *fun*. Out of everyone in my new family, she's the one I love spending time with. It's like everything terrible, all the bad things that have happened to me all fade away when I'm with her, and I love that about her. I wouldn't mind spending all of my time with her.

She's so happy.

For a moment I watch her wrestle out a puzzle box, then I get up to help her. Together, we pull it free from the stack, then I hand it to her to carry into the kitchen. That's where she likes to be—right in the thick of it with her family.

I liked it too, for a while. But now Mom doesn't seem to want me around. It makes me sad, how she was so happy to have me here and now she isn't. But what do I do about it? I can't ask her what's wrong, why she doesn't seem to want me in the house any longer. What if she told me? What if she came clean with me and it wasn't something I did, something I could fix, it was the fact that I exist?

I don't think I'd be able to handle it. It's one thing to upset someone, to do something and know that your actions hurt them, but it's another thing entirely to simply exist and have someone not like that about you.

It was probably too much to ask for her to love me the way she loves Anna.

"Brudder!" Anna calls me from the kitchen, snapping me out of my thoughts. I'd honestly not realized I'm still standing right by the game closet in the living room. I do that sometimes, get lost in my own thoughts, but she wants me to play with her, so I walk towards the kitchen.

As I do, my mind races. Will Mom be in there? Maybe she was having a bad morning and snapped at me by accident. Maybe she'll apologize, pull me into a hug and tell me how grateful she is that I'm here with her family.

Maybe she'll tell me she loves me.

That's all I wanted from my biological mom, but she couldn't give it to me, could she?

And now look where she is.

39

ZOE

Sunday March 19

The rest of the day yesterday passed uneventfully. I kept an eye on Micah and Anna because I didn't want to leave them alone. Each time I got close to them, though, Micah would stop talking. It was like he didn't want me to hear what the two of them were chatting about. Did it drive me nuts?

Yes.

Was there anything I could do about it?

Not really.

Now Ethan and Anna have gone downtown to our favorite bakery to bring some donuts back for breakfast. I wanted to go with him—I *love* going there, love smelling the yeast, the melted chocolate. I love seeing the cookies being frosted, thick whorls of it piled high, sure to cause a sugar rush in any kid lucky enough to get one to eat, but instead I'm here.

At home.

With Micah.

He didn't want to go. He was sullen last night after dinner while Ethan gave Anna her bath. I didn't want to talk to him either, so we sat in silence in the living room, me doing my best to read a book, him staring off into space.

"Don't you have homework?" I'd asked once, desperate to fill the silence even though I didn't want to talk to him.

He'd leveled his gaze on me and reminded me that he'd come home early from school Friday because he was sick.

Yeah, *sick*.

So now he's in the living room, again, and I'm in the kitchen, looking out the window, waiting for Ethan and Anna to get back. Right now it seems like my daughter is the only person Micah likes, the only one who can even make him crack a smile. He still calls me *Mom*, still looks at me sometimes like he's wanting to say something to me, but I need space from him.

It's terrible, but the only thing I can think of when I look at him are the pictures he downloaded onto his computer. How he's been watching me. *Researching* me.

"You're a better mother than she ever was," he'd said to me once, and I'd smiled, swelled with pride before the thought hit me that for me to be that person something had to have happened to his mom. Hearing that from a child, even a child I didn't carry myself, made me feel proud. It made me feel like I was doing something right, like I was to be envied, not just a *good* mother, but a *better* one.

And now the thought makes my skin crawl.

Time ticks by slowly and I glance at my wrist when my

Fitbit buzzes, trying to convince me to move. Apparently I still have ten minutes left in the hour to get my steps, and I turn away from the window, walking over to the cupboard to set the table.

It's loud, me moving the dishes around, clattering through the silverware drawer. No matter how many times I ask Ethan to put the spoons with the spoons, the forks with the forks, it's like he can't get it through his head. Half of the time it's a jumble in there. I remarked once that I hoped he remembered where to put organs back when he was operating.

That joke didn't go over well.

After I dig out what I need, I finish setting the table. Walk back to the window. I feel like a war widow, looking out the window, eyeballing the rolling water, the high waves, the dark gray color of the sea, looking for a ship, a mast, anything that will give me peace that my husband is fine.

A BMW. I'm staring out the window looking for a stupid BMW, all because I'm too nervous of the young boy in the other room to concentrate on anything else.

Heaving a sigh, I push away from the window. My Fitbit buzzes again, a celebration of digital confetti appearing on the face, congratulating me for moving the required amount.

Micah hasn't made a peep from the living room. I debate with myself about going in there, trying to talk to him. Ethan played everything up like it was no big deal, like he's a troubled kid who needs a little help. I want to believe him, I want to trust that my husband would know his biological child well enough to guarantee that Micah's no threat.

But we don't know him, do we? Until last week we didn't even know he existed.

Still, he's going to be here for a while. Years, probably,

unless he goes to college early. Getting him help is the most important thing, but I don't think he'll be receptive to talking to someone unless he knows it's coming, unless he's been prepared.

I sigh. Rub my hands together.

It's silly, isn't it, to be so nervous about approaching another person? I've never felt this way about anyone, not even when I first met Ethan and thought he was so handsome. I walked right up to him in the break room and introduced myself, omitting the fact that I was pretty sure I would be his future wife.

And now look where I am.

Too afraid to talk to a teenager who's in my own house. Who sleeps in the room next to me. Who plays with my daughter and calls me "Mom."

Well, no more. Ethan made it clear that Micah is staying and that he doesn't think his son is a threat. I'm not so sure about that second fact, but I'm going to find out for myself. To steel myself, I take a deep breath, holding the air in my lungs until I feel like I'm going to pass out, then walk confidently from the kitchen into the living room.

Only he's not in here.

40

ZOE

"Micah?" I call as I walk through the living room, looking behind the furniture, checking to make sure he's not digging through the game closet and I somehow missed him. "Micah, where are you?"

No response. The house is silent, oppressive. It feels like it's weighing down on me, like the weight of it is going to be enough to crush me to the ground. I don't stop moving, don't give the silence a chance to do that.

Backtracking, I turn, not into the kitchen, but check the small bathroom right off the living room. Even as I reach for the door, though, I know he's not in here. The light is off, the door cracked. He's not here, not in the living room, not with me in the kitchen.

He's so sneaky.

I feel a chill dance up my spine and I shiver, wrapping my arms around myself in a bid to stay warm as I leave the bathroom then walk to the stairs. The second floor is dark, making it look like the staircase disappears into nothing, and I hesitate, my hand on the railing before I start ascending.

"Micah?" His name leaves my lips before I'm halfway up the stairs. I hesitate, hoping he's going to answer me. I don't want to look for him, don't want to have to complete some stressful game of hide and seek to try to find him, don't want to wander around my house wondering where he is, what he's doing. I hate the fact that he left the living room and I didn't even know he was on the move.

What else don't I know?

I reach the landing on the second floor and that's when I hear it—crying.

Guilt washes over me, the wave of it so heavy I almost sink to my knees. I feel weak, like everything in the house is stronger than me right now, but as much as I'd love to turn and go back to the first floor, I don't allow myself. Instead, I push on, focused on getting into Micah's room, focused on finding him there, trying to comfort him.

How do I comfort someone I believe to be a killer?

Pushing that thought from my mind, I push open Micah's door. "Micah, will you talk to me?" My voice is quiet. It shakes. Even my heart, which is pounding hard, feels like it's trembling, like it can't keep a steady beat.

He's not in here. The room is empty, silent. Now that I'm farther down the hall, I can tell where the crying is coming from and I turn around, hurrying into the bathroom.

"Micah." I don't hesitate when I push open the bathroom door partly because I need to see him here, need to know I found him, but also partly because I don't want to see my hand hover in front of my face, don't want to see how it trembles.

He's on the floor, his knees up to his chest, his forehead

resting on them. *Gosh, he looks so young.* His arms are wrapped around his legs, his hands tight, the tendons in the backs of them popping out.

"Micah." I drop down to my knees next to him, unsure of what to do. Before this, before I knew all the things he'd been doing, all the online stalking he'd done, I would have pulled him to me, held him close, let him cry into my chest. I wouldn't have worried about his tears soaking my shirt or what kind of danger I might be in.

Now, though, I rest my hand on his shoulder. It's stiff, my hand, and it feels wooden, but I hope he can feel the heat from my touch and will get some comfort from it.

"Why don't you want me here?" Micah speaks without looking up at me, so his voice is muffled.

Even though I don't want to admit to myself that I know what he said, I can't hide from the truth. I thought pulling away from him was the best thing for my own safety and mental health.

I never thought he'd pick up on it. I didn't consider how it would make him feel.

"Micah, I don't know what you're talking about. I'm busy, but I'm not pulling away from you."

He jerks away from me. When he lifts his head from his knees, I'm not surprised to see his eyes are puffy. Red. His cheeks are wet with tears and he exhales hard, the sound wet.

"I'm not stupid. I thought you loved me."

This is it. I'm at the precipice and it would be too easy to accidentally mess this up. "I'm so glad you're here, Micah," I say. "Why don't you come downstairs and we'll get you cleaned up? Ethan and Anna will be home with breakfast soon."

It's important I get him downstairs as quickly as possible. Even though he might feel good sitting up here crying, I need to make sure Ethan doesn't see him so upset. He'll want to know why Micah's crying and if Micah tells him I haven't been kind to him, that I've pushed him away, then my husband will get angry. And rightfully so.

"You'd be happier if I stayed up here."

The words are a dare. The way he looks at me, how he's holding his jaw tight, his head slightly tilted to the side... it's all a dare, him wanting to know what I'm going to say in response. He wants to catch me out, to hear me lie to his face. That, or he wants me to be honest, to throw the truth at him, barbs sticking into his skin, hurting him.

"I wouldn't," I say, and I muster up all the honesty I possibly can. "I would be much happier if you came downstairs with me, Micah."

He examines me. I feel him looking into me like he'll be able to uncover whether or not I'm lying to him, and I hold fast to my conviction. He doesn't have to know that the reason I'd be happier if he came downstairs with me is because then Ethan wouldn't ask questions about why he was upstairs. Him coming downstairs and cleaning himself up before my family gets home is the best outcome I can see right now.

"Fine." He stands, unfolding and towering over me, his movement so fluid that I gape up at him from the floor, barely able to stand up before he's halfway out the door. He moves quickly now, like he's on a mission, and I hurry down the stairs after him.

"If you come with me into the kitchen I'll get a cool rag for you. Help you clean up," I say, but I'm speaking to his back as he walks into the kitchen and to the sink. Moving as if this was all his idea, he wets a rag and wipes his face. Tosses it back in the sink.

Goes to sit at the table.

"Happy?" The glare he gives me tells me he is anything but. His body language radiates his displeasure, how he wishes he were anywhere else right now, or with anyone else.

I nod. There's nothing for me to say. Only the sound of Ethan's car in the garage makes us look away from each other.

Thank goodness. I need him here to act as a buffer. I need to be able to keep Anna close to me, keep her safe. Even though I should be perfectly able to handle Micah on my own, that's the last thing I want.

He hears the sound of the garage door and turns away from me, but not before I see him put a smile on his face. It's creepy, how easily he can cover up his true feelings, how quickly he can hide what he's thinking so that Ethan won't know it.

A shiver races up my arms and I rub my hands up and down them absentmindedly.

Tomorrow's Monday. I have to make it through today and then I'll have some alone time at the house. I know I shouldn't snoop, I know leaving well enough alone is the best option for me to keep from going crazy worrying about Micah, but I'm going to do it.

I'm going to find out everything I can about this boy, and I'm going to do it behind Ethan's back so he won't try to stop me. Until then, I have to pretend everything is fine.

I'm so close to the truth. I know it.

41

ZOE

Monday March 20

My mask doesn't drop until I'm back in the house Monday morning after dropping off Anna and Micah. I glance down at my watch and check the time, heaving a sigh of relief when I see that I have over five hours until I have to pick up Anna. Normally I never sign her up for the lunch bunch aftercare at her preschool, but I did today, just so I could have a little extra time.

She was excited to get to spend more time with her friends. I'm excited to get to spend more time snooping without having to worry about anyone seeing what I'm doing.

"Alright, Micah," I say, rubbing my hands together and striding to the stairs, "let's see what else you have hidden in your room." Even though this is my house and I should feel comfortable in every room of it, I still hover at his doorway, glancing inside almost like I expect him to still be there.

But he's not. I dropped him off. Watched his smile slide off his face as he turned from Anna to me. He likes her, he really does, and there's part of me that doesn't appreciate how close he feels to her. Or how willing she is to drop everything to play with him. I tried to keep them apart yesterday afternoon, but it was impossible, especially when I had to make meals and clean up and do laundry...

My thoughts fade as I walk into Micah's room. It hasn't changed much since I was in here to snoop the first time, but now I know what to look for. I rush for his bed and throw back the covers, half expecting his laptop to be missing.

But it's right there.

"Thank goodness," I whisper, pulling it onto my lap as I sit down. It fires right up but this time a small box appears asking me for a password, and my heart sinks. "You've got to be kidding."

I close my eyes, tap my finger against my chin. The implication of him password-protecting his laptop isn't lost on me. He obviously figured out somehow that I'd been in his room looking through his things. That should bother me more than it does, but what upsets me right now is the fact that I don't know what his password might be.

PASSWORD.

No dice.

That's it. That's one of the most common passwords people use, but it was too much to hope it would be what I'd need to unlock his computer. I don't know much about him, so how in the world am I to guess what he might use to lock up his secrets?

My name.

My fingers feel clumsy as I type in ZOE, but it's too short. Relief flows through me and I exhale hard, grateful that he couldn't possibly use my name as his password. I'm about to close the computer and move on to looking under his bed when it hits me.

ANNA.

The computer thinks for a moment then the screen clears. *Anna.* He used my daughter's name as his password. I have to press my fingers against my mouth and close my eyes as I try to fight down the nausea billowing in my stomach. I knew he liked her, knew he thought she was more fun than anyone else in the family, but that's weird, right?

It's obsessive. It's over the top.

I'm nervous as I click through his most recent searches. They're all related to schoolwork and while I should feel relieved that he hasn't searched for anything else that might creep me out, I'm a little disappointed. Maybe, with undeniable proof, I could convince Ethan that Micah's a problem. I could get rid of him.

But there's nothing here. I close the computer, put it back in the bed, and remake it, then fall to my knees.

Nothing under the bed.

In the closet, then.

My heart slams hard as I open his closet door, although,

what do I expect? Rita's body to be hanging here next to his shirts?

The thought makes me laugh and I cover my mouth, trying to prevent the sound from escaping as if there were anyone else here who might hear what I'm doing. Still, it feels strange to laugh about something like that, strange when this is more serious than I want to admit.

But there's nothing out of place. No personal artifacts, nothing that would make me look twice. Even the backpack he showed up with when he came here is gone. I know we didn't throw it away; I wouldn't do that to him, wouldn't get rid of his past like that.

So then where is it?

I leave his room, mulling over the problem as I walk back downstairs. In the kitchen I pause, leaning against the counter. Sunlight streams through the window above the sink, a clear sign that it's going to be a gorgeous day. I'd much rather be outside working in the garden or taking a walk at the park, but instead I'm going to be stuck in here, doing everything I can to figure out the truth about my husband's son.

It's crazy. If I were watching a movie and the heroine was acting like this, I'd wonder what in the world was her problem. I'd scream at the screen to get her husband on the same page as her, or to put her foot down and get rid of the boy.

But this is real life, not TV. Nothing about this is perfect or planned out.

And I feel like this is all on me. This is something I brought on myself because I couldn't say no when Micah turned up on our front porch looking for all the world like he didn't have a friend to help him. I made Ethan help him and now I have to live with that decision.

Unless I find something that proves Micah is more dangerous than even I could imagine.

"So that's why you need to stop staring out the window and imagining you're outside," I tell myself, pushing away from the counter. "You need to find that backpack because that might be the key to this all."

I don't know that for sure, but it makes sense to me. If I were trying to hide something from someone, I'd want to tuck it in a personal item, somewhere other people might not look. His filthy backpack fits the bill perfectly.

So where would he put it? It wasn't in his room, but that doesn't mean it was thrown away. For a moment, I consider calling Ethan and asking him, but not only would I have to go through Bonnie first, but I'd have to explain to him why I wanted to know and he'd get mad at me for seeing a problem that didn't exist.

That's a no-go.

Then it hits me. I'll look in the one place Ethan puts things when he wants to keep them out of sight so I don't worry about them. Sure, I might see them out of the corner of my eye, but when things are relegated to the garage, they often go there to die, to be ignored, to sit there on a shelf until he gets a bee in his bonnet and cleans it all out, pulling all of our secrets out onto the driveway for the neighbors to see before loading them up and going to the dump.

The garage. That's it.

If Micah's backpack is still around, and if it has anything in it that will help me prove to my husband how creepy and possibly dangerous his son is, it'll be in there.

I'm full of resolve now as I hurry to the garage. Swing open the door. Flick on the light. My car is right in the middle, right where I like to park during the day when

Ethan is working, so I have plenty of room to walk around and look at the shelves.

Luckily for me, Ethan organized this place recently. He made a dump trip about a month ago, so the clutter and crap that might make this job harder is all gone, someone else's problem.

That's why it takes me less than five minutes to find what I'm looking for.

Right there, on the top shelf. I almost didn't recognize it except one strap is hanging down over the edge of the shelf, looking out of place among the plastic storage bins. It's tucked up high where both Ethan and Micah can easily reach it but I have to grab the step stool, hauling it around my car before carefully setting it up.

If there are answers to how I can get rid of Micah, they're in there.

I know it.

42

ZOE

Even on the step stool, I have to stretch high, my fingers brushing against the backpack strap once, twice, three times before I finally hook a finger around it and yank it down. It slips off the shelf easily and I reach up with my other hand, protecting my head as I finally grab it.

"There you are," I mutter, grinning for a moment before I'm hit with the smell. "Oh, God." I adjust my grip, pinching it between my thumb and forefinger with one hand and holding it out from my body as I step down from the stool and drop it to the garage floor.

In my mind, I'd pictured taking it into the house and putting it on the kitchen table so I could spread out and take my time looking through it. I'd make a cup of coffee and enjoy the fact that I had a few hours left to figure out how I could convince Ethan we needed to get rid of Micah.

But this thing isn't going anywhere near my kitchen table, not the way it smells. It's funny, I noticed a sour smell when Micah arrived that first night, but it's like the smell has intensified, almost cooking and increasing in the garage.

"Let's do this," I say, crouching down next to the back-pack. My thighs are going to burn when I stand back up but I hope this will all be worth it, that I'll get the answers I need.

I unzip the big pocket first. The way the backpack has slumped to the floor makes me think there might be some-thing in there, and I move quickly, pulling the zipper open in one smooth motion and then flipping the front of the back-pack down to get a look inside.

Yeah, there's something in here. I reach in, nervous now, wondering for a moment if I should put on gloves, but then I'm grabbing the fabric and pulling it out, putting it on the concrete floor next to me.

It takes a minute for me to figure out what it is. It's a shirt —that much is clear—but I have to unfold it and smooth it out to see what it is. There's no way this was Micah's; it's much too small, much too feminine.

It's Rita's.

That realization hits me and I rock back on my heels, exhaling hard. It's a V-neck, with crystals around the neck. The sleeves are flutter sleeves and it's cut short, like a crop top. The bright blue color it was originally is faded and dull. Even though I've never met Rita and I never will now, I'm sure this is hers.

Why does Micah have it? Why would he bring it from his home and keep it in his backpack?

Like the majority of women in the United States, I love serial killer documentaries. How many times have I heard the narrator talking about the trophies killers like to keep from their victims? Is that what this is—a trophy? Did Micah kill his mother and then bring her shirt here so he could remember her?

Or is there an easier explanation? Maybe that he brought his mother's shirt because he loved her? Sure, she was a terrible mom, but she was still his mom. Maybe he didn't kill her. Maybe he wanted to have something of hers when he left, in case he missed her.

I don't know. Again, I want to call Ethan, but now telling him what I'm doing would upset him. He'd hate me for going behind his back, for not trusting his son.

And, you know what? I hate me too. I hate that I'm crouched here, in my garage, wondering what this shirt meant to Micah. Guilt washes over me as I sit here, trying to figure out Micah's motives in bringing the shirt.

"Put yourself in his shoes," I say, closing my eyes and breathing hard. "Your mom is a terrible mom. You think she might be dead and so you flee the house to go to your biological father's home. Maybe you bring her shirt because it smells like her."

I open my eyes. Look at the piece of clothing. Yeah, no way am I putting my nose anywhere near that and taking a nice big whiff.

Sitting all the way back on the floor, I try to relax. There's still one more pocket in his backpack, and I toe the shirt out of the way so I can unzip the small pocket.

This one jams and I yank hard on it, wincing a little at the sound of popping threads. It's a good thing Micah isn't relying on this backpack for school. It's also a good thing he doesn't keep it in his room where he can look at it. I don't know how well he knows it, but the last thing I want is for him to figure out I was digging through his stuff.

Again.

I'm pretty sure he knows about the computer. Why else would he have put a password on it? There's no other explanation for that. It would also explain the scowling, how he stares at me now like he can't stand me, like being in the same room with me is enough to put his teeth on edge.

Or maybe he's picked up on how unhappy I am to have him here. There's a bit of guilt attached to that thought but I push it away as I carefully open the second pocket. It's dark in there and there's no way I'm plunging my hand into it without having an idea what might be lurking inside.

I have to angle the backpack to allow enough light to enter the pocket so I can see that it's empty. Sighing, I sit back and drop the backpack back down to the floor. Disappointment washes over me like a wave, but what was I expecting?

A murder weapon? Did I really think there might be a bloody knife in his backpack? I mean, Micah is a teenager and his brain isn't fully formed yet, but that would definitely land him on the Top Ten Stupidest Criminals list. Bringing his mother's murder weapon into our home would be insane.

But at the same time, I don't know if I'd have been surprised. I mean, come on. I've seen those lists. Murderers do some stupid things that I want to believe I'd never be dumb enough to do. Then again, it's easy to be judgmental about someone else's decisions when I'm in my pjs watching from the comfort of my home.

So nothing here. No murder weapon. No written confession, not that I actually thought there would be something like that. Still, a note, maybe, any kind of proof that he killed Rita would have perfectly fit what I was looking for.

My back aches and I stretch before bending back down

for the backpack. I don't want to touch Rita's shirt, don't want to think that it might have been one of the last things she wore, but I still pick it up and cram it back into the backpack. Better that Micah doesn't see it lying around.

Better still that Ethan doesn't see it and realize I'm still trying to figure out if his son is a murderer.

Just as I'm about to clamber back up on the step stool to tuck the backpack where it belongs, I hear something from inside the house. The sound is faint and, at first, I worry that I'm hearing things that aren't there.

Stress will do that to you, you know. It will make it difficult for you to rationalize between what is real and what's fake, but I'm sure that's my phone.

Anna.

I glance down at the backpack in my hand, then drop it on the floor. Then, like someone on a top ten list of stupid criminals, I kick it to the side before running into the house to grab my phone.

43

MICAH

"Sick again?" Mom doesn't turn to look at me while she speaks. Her hands are tight on the wheel, her eyes on the road ahead of us. I see how her pulse beats in her neck and I realize how angry she is with me calling her again and making her come pick me up.

But this time I honestly was sick. This time I threw up, not just on the floor and my desk, but down my shirt, the stench of it making me feel like I'm going to throw up again every time I take a breath.

That's why the windows are down. That's why Mom didn't hug me when she came to get me. Or, at least, that's what I'm going to tell myself.

"I threw up," I say, almost defensively. She can't pretend I'm not really sick when the evidence of it is all the way down my shirt. "I didn't mean to."

"I know." A heavy sigh. "Do you think you're going to have to throw up before we get home?"

I look down at the plastic bag in my lap before answering. The nurse had handed it to me but kept her distance as she did. Maybe she didn't want my germs. Or maybe she didn't want to smell me.

"I don't know," I say, trying to be honest. "My stomach is all tight and gross."

"Well, I'm sorry you feel like that. I think a shower and straight to bed is the best option, don't you?" She turns a little, barely enough to glance at me, like she's checking for my agreement.

So I nod.

"Good. You can get as much rest as possible and then maybe you'll feel well enough to go to school tomorrow."

Oh, no. "The nurse said I can't come back until I haven't thrown up for twenty-four hours." I feel terrible telling her that, but how I feel is made even worse by the way her shoulders sag forward with the news.

What did I do to make her dislike me so much? I want to ask her that, want to know why she went from wanting me in the house to acting like she can't wait until I'm gone. She had to have been on my computer. It's the only thing I can think of, the only thing that would change how she felt about me so drastically.

But I wasn't doing anything wrong. I was researching her. I wanted to make sure she would be a better mother than the one I had, and who wouldn't do that? A new mother is a big commitment and it wasn't one I was going to take very lightly. I had to make sure she was the better choice.

And I thought she was. I really did.

We stop in the driveway and she turns off the car. "I'm going to park out here to keep the garage clean. You can take off your shirt on the porch. That way you won't accidentally drip."

Drip? I look down at myself. Gross. Yeah, fair. I might not

want to strip on the front porch but I don't blame her for not wanting me to stroll through the house. Still, I turn in my seat, looking at the houses around us.

"They're working. Nobody will see you."

"Thanks." I get out, feeling a bit woozy for a moment, but that passes. Maybe this is going to be a one-and-done thing. The fresh air definitely makes me feel less pukey. I felt fine after breakfast, so I don't know what it was that I ate, but it had to be something that didn't sit right.

Mom leads me up to the house without saying another word.

I follow her, taking deep breaths as I do, enjoying how much better I feel. Getting out of that small nurse's office helped too, I think. It was like I couldn't take a full breath in there, like all I was breathing in was someone else's sick, but now that's passed and I can actually gulp down clean air.

"Strip here." Mom has the door open and she eyeballs me. "You can leave any dirty clothes and I'll put them in the wash. When I hear you get out of the shower I'll come up and check on you."

I know she's mad at me, or at least that something's wrong between the two of us, but I still don't want her to go. I reach for her but drop my hand before touching her arm. "What are you going to be doing?"

She frowns. "I have a few things to clean up. Now, go. You'll feel a lot better when you get cleaned up and in bed. Trust me."

I do trust her. And, because I want her to like me again, I'm willing to do whatever it will take.

"I trust you." I offer her a smile. Maybe we're turning a corner. Maybe, even though she was obviously upset with me for a while, that's passed. She's my mom now, so she can't be mad at me forever.

But she doesn't return my smile. She stares at me then gives her head a little shake like she can't quite believe what's happening. My stomach twists as she turns away from me and walks into the house, closing the door hard behind her.

I know I need to strip down and get in the shower like she told me. I know I should follow her directions but I don't get it. I don't get what I did wrong.

It feels stupid to be this upset about it, to care this much when it's pretty clear she doesn't, but I can't help it. Even though she makes me angry with how she's treating me, even though she doesn't seem to care about me nearly as much as I care about her, I still want her to love me.

I pull off my shirt, feeling miserable again, and drop it to the porch. It's stupid. Stupid of me to feel like this about someone who doesn't care for me. But what's more stupid is that if I had the chance to make her see that I'm special, that I'm worth caring about, that she should be my mom, I'd take it in a heartbeat.

It doesn't matter what it is.

I still want Zoe for my mom. And I know I'd do whatever it took to prove that to her. If only I got the chance.

44

ZOE

How could I have been so stupid leaving Micah's backpack on the garage floor when I left the house to get him from school? It was sloppy, that's what it was. But at least I could park out in the driveway and tell him I didn't want him to get the garage dirty.

He seemed to buy it, but I can only imagine how upset with me he'd be if he'd seen that I'd been snooping through his things. That's definitely not a scene I want to have play out. Thank goodness Anna isn't here. And thank goodness I realized my mistake before he had a chance to see it.

Now I hurry to the garage but I wait by the door until he enters the house and heads upstairs. I don't think he'd come into the garage behind me to see what I'm doing, but what if he did? What if he snuck up behind me—because that's how he tends to move, right? What if I didn't hear him until he was right there, putting two and two together, figuring out what I did?

No, I can't have that.

So when his shower clicks on, I breathe a sigh of relief and hurry into the garage. The backpack is right where I left it and I grab it by a strap, ignoring how bad it smells, and climb up the step stool. It will only take a moment to swing it up to the top shelf and I do that, releasing it at the last second so it lands right where I need it to.

But it falls back down.

"Dammit." Hopping down from the stool, I pick it back up. I must not have thrown it hard enough, so it landed on the shelf but the weight of the straps pulled it back down. I'm moving faster now, still trying to stay calm but knowing full well that I need to get this taken care of quickly.

This time I heave the backpack harder. It slams into the back of the shelf, the straps completely out of reach, and I sigh, rubbing my hands together. Great. This is great. It's out of the way, although not quite where Ethan put it when he threw it up there in the first place. If Ethan were to pay attention to how far back it is, he might realize someone was messing with it and then put it back, but I don't think he'll notice. When he gets home in the evenings he's in such a hurry he hardly glances around.

And since he cleaned out the garage a short while ago, he won't have any reason to be investigating the shelves. I'm in the clear.

Right as I'm about to hop down from the step stool, though, something catches my eye on the top shelf. I didn't see it there before, so when the backpack fell down it must have dislodged it. Frowning, I tilt my head back, stand up on my tiptoes.

What is it?

There's something about the shape of it that gives me pause, and then it hits me. Small. Rectangular.

"Did Micah have a phone?" The words leave my lips before I even have time to realize what I'm looking at. It's definitely a phone, tucked way high up on the shelf. I have to stretch to even touch it, but I push it back from the edge.

"Think," I say, hopping down. In the corner of the garage are some golf clubs Ethan bought a few summers ago after swearing he was going to take up the sport. Honestly, I think he's only been out to play once since then, but right now I'm grateful he has them. I grab a club and hurry back to the stool.

It's hard to angle my body the right way to touch the phone, but I do, and the last thing I see before it falls into my waiting hand is the pink case.

Dropping the club, I turn the phone over and over in my hand. A pink case.

Micah doesn't wear pink. I took him shopping and everything he picked out was black or green or blue. Honestly, I think the boy might be physically ill if I tried to put him in pink.

I find the power button on the side and press it, but the phone doesn't light up. It's dead, the battery probably drained from sitting in our garage for so long.

"I have a charger," I whisper, then climb down from the step stool. My hand feels numb and I grip the phone with both hands so I don't drop it. "I have a charger and then I can charge it and see whose phone it is." I think for a moment about what I said, then push the thought away. "It's Rita's, it has to be. But why would Micah have it? Why would he take his mom's phone? Why would she leave him with it?"

Because he killed her.

The little voice in the back of my head screams the answer at me but I don't want to acknowledge it. The phone feels like a bomb, like it's going to explode in my hand if I'm not careful. My thumb presses down on the side button again, in case it turns on this time.

No dice.

I stumble to the kitchen door and lean in, tilting my head a bit so I can listen for the shower. It's running, which means Micah is busy, at least for a little while. I know I promised him I'd go up and check on him after he gets out of the shower, but I have to take care of this first.

I have to know.

There's a junk drawer by the kitchen sink. Everyone has one of those, right? A place where everything that doesn't have a home goes, a place of old chargers, rubber bands, business cards from people you'll never see again, chopsticks from the takeout place in town, even a few address labels.

That's where I head, my head pounding the entire time. The phone clatters when I drop it to the counter and I wince, looking back up above my head like I fully expect Micah to have heard me.

The shower's still on.

We have four old chargers, a massive snarl of black cable tucked in the back of the drawer. I yank it out, ignoring the pen that flies free and clatters to the floor. My heart beats hard as I try the first charger, then the second, finally the third. This one slips into the charging port on the phone with a click and I exhale hard, then plug it into the wall.

How long will it take to charge? I have no idea, no clue about how long I'll need to leave it alone until I can turn it on and see what's on the phone. Maybe there's evidence on there. I'm sure it's Rita's phone—I can feel it in my bones— but even though I know that, I'm honestly not entirely sure what I'm looking for on it.

I need something that will prove Micah killed her. It's pretty damning that he brought her phone with him to our house, isn't it?

I pause, listening.

The shower's still running.

Anxious now, I press the button on the side of the phone. A small battery symbol appears on the screen, slowly filling up before starting over, but that's it. There's no way this thing is turning on right now. Or anytime soon.

Ethan. I have to call Ethan.

I know I promised myself I wouldn't bother him at work anymore, but this isn't something I want to handle on my own. Once I get the proof that Micah killed Rita... well, then I'm going to be stuck in the house with a killer.

My phone is in my purse and I lunge for it, tapping the screen until it rings. I press it against my ear, closing my eyes and saying a little prayer that Ethan picks up. That it's my husband, not—

"Hi, Zoe." Bonnie sounds so chipper I could scream. "You barely missed Ethan; he's walking away now."

Then why didn't he pick up the phone?

"Bonnie, it's an emergency. I need to talk to him. Now."

"An emergency?" She gasps like she can't believe it's her lucky day. "Ethan! It's Zoe! An emergency." When she speaks again, her voice drips with interest. "Do you want to tell me what's going on, Zoe? He's coming back but I can tell him right now if you want."

"Let me talk to my husband, Bonnie." I hate this woman. Hate her fake concern, hate how she is always there when I need to talk to Ethan, like some sort of gatekeeper in a video game, someone I need to destroy to get past her. I hate how she always seems to know when I'm upset, how she gets to spend more time with Ethan than I do. If I hadn't quit my job I'd still be at the hospital, not here, not with Micah upstairs.

"Zoe?" Ethan now. He sounds concerned and I melt back against the counter, grateful for the support it offers me. "What's going on? Bonnie said there was an emergency."

"Ethan." My voice comes out in a squeak and I clear my throat to try again. "Ethan, I need you home. I found a phone."

A pause. "A phone?"

"A pink one. In the garage. I think it's Rita's. I think Micah killed her."

"Have you called the police?" Of course he'd ask that. He's so good about doing things by the book.

"No, I called you. I did plug it in, though. It was dead but I have it charging so we can see what's on it. But it was out there with Micah's backpack. It was hidden, and I think—"

"I'm coming home right now. Wait for me. I'll handle everything when I get there. It'll all be fine."

"Do you think he killed her?" I whisper the words in case Micah's leaving the shower running to throw me off the track, so he can sneak downstairs without me realizing he's behind me. "Do you think that's why he brought her phone here, as a trophy of some sort?"

"I don't know, Zoe, but let me help you. Let me look on the phone. You shouldn't have to see anything terrible."

I glance at the phone. It's taking forever to charge and I still have to go upstairs and pretend Micah doesn't freak me out. "Deal," I say, "but hurry."

The shower clicks off. It feels like ice slides down my spine and I shiver, gripping the phone tightly.

"I'm on my way. Wait for me." He hangs up.

Automatically, I go to put my phone on the counter, but

then I change my mind and slip it into my back pocket. I have to go upstairs and make sure Micah goes to bed. I told him I'd do that and the alternative, that he'd come down here to look for me and see Rita's phone plugged in, terrifies me.

It hits me that I need to hide the phone, and I grab a towel, tossing it over the phone to cover the pink.

There. That's hidden. Even if Micah were to come downstairs, he wouldn't see it.

Now I have to go up there. I have to tuck him into bed. I have to pretend I care.

Then Ethan will be here and he'll take care of everything.

45

ZOE

"Micah?" I have déjà vu of walking through the house looking for him and I pause at the top of the stairs to clear away the thought. Focus on what's happening now, not on what happened before. "Are you feeling better?"

"I'm in bed."

He's fast. That, or I stood down there in the kitchen working up the nerve to walk up here for longer than I realized. That's probably what it was. Time has no meaning right now. Everything feels slippery, like I'm in a fugue state and things are happening around me and to me but I'm not actually interacting with the world.

It's uncomfortable.

"Oh, good," I say, forcing myself to walk to his room. "Did the shower help you feel better? Do you need anything?" I stand in the doorway, unable to get closer to him. He looks so small in the bed, with the covers pulled up to his chin, but I know better, don't I?

I've seen how tall he is when he stands up, how he

towers over me, how large his hands are. If I had any doubt in my mind that a boy could kill his mother, it's gone now. Looking at Micah and knowing the truth about how creepy he is has completely changed my mind about everything.

I thought I knew how the world worked.

I was wrong.

"I'm fine. Just tired. Thank you." His voice is small. It seems incongruous with how grown up he looks. "I want to sleep."

"Sleep is good." My hand is on the doorknob already, I'm so prepared to pull it shut, put this behind me. When I close my eyes, I can picture Ethan in his car, zipping along the road, hurrying home to help me out. He won't leave me here to handle this on my own.

"I'll see you when I get up." He's still looking at me expectantly, but I don't know what he wants me to do. Hug him? The thought chills me.

When I realize he's still watching me, his face turned towards me, his eyes locked on me, I try to cover up my involuntary shudder. "I'm so sorry you don't feel good. I'll check on you later. Stay right here."

"Thank you." This time, he shifts a little, tucking the blanket around himself. "I'll see you soon."

"Yep." My mouth is dry and it's the only thing I can make myself say. Backing up slowly, I close the door, then exhale hard in relief and lean against it.

Ethan should be close to our neighborhood by now. He's a safe driver, always has been, but I can't imagine him taking his time when he knows how scared I am. He'll be pushing the limits of his car, sliding through stop signs, maybe even running a red light.

Honestly, I don't care what he has to do to get here, as long as he's here before Micah decides to come downstairs.

I creep away from his room, not wanting to make any noise, then hurry downstairs, straight to the kitchen to check the phone. Still charging, the little battery on the screen slowly filling up then emptying before starting over. It can't take much longer, right? This has to hurry up.

In case Micah comes downstairs, I put the towel back over the phone and walk to the front door to wait for Ethan. I'm still parked in the driveway so he'll have to park behind me. He won't like that, but I don't think I can pull my car into the garage right now. My hands are shaking and my feet feel like they're encased in concrete.

Two minutes later he pulls in. Just as I thought, he's driving faster than normal. I watch, pleased, as he slams on the brakes behind my car. There's a loud bang as he closes his door, then he runs up the walkway to me, pulling me into his arms.

"Where is it?" It's the first thing he asks, not *how are you* or *has Micah done anything to you* and it strikes me as odd, but I guess I never told him his son is home from school.

"The kitchen," I say, pulling back, "but listen, you need to know—"

He's already running past me and I stop talking. Close the front door. Follow him. Even though I'm still scared, even though Micah could come downstairs at any moment, Ethan is here. He won't let anything bad happen to me.

Ethan turns a slow circle in the kitchen, his brow furrowed. "Zoe? Where?"

"Under the towel," I say, grabbing it from the phone and pressing the button on the side. The pink case is so bright, so girly, that I wonder for a moment what Rita was like to have chosen this phone case. Mine is black. Boring. Predictable, but not flashy.

"Is it turning on?" He's at my side, reaching for the phone. I watch as he lifts it from my fingers at the same moment the screen flashes.

"It's on!" Excitement rushes through me. "Thank God! I was worried it wouldn't ever turn on and we wouldn't know for sure, but it's on! Ethan, this is great. We can look through it, call the cops. You need to know about Micah."

I wait for my husband to look at me. This is important and I don't like the fact that he won't pay attention to what I'm saying. I want all of his attention, but he's staring at the screen as it loads.

So I change tactics. "Why do you think he brought it here with him?" I touch Ethan's shoulder. "Do you think it was on purpose? Or do you think he panicked?"

"I don't know." Ethan pauses. Sucks his teeth. He taps the screen, trying to open her messaging app, but the phone is slow to respond. "This stupid thing is so old. Why won't it open up?"

"Give it time." I look over his shoulder, grabbing his arm for support. I need to touch him, to feel his muscles, to convince myself that he can handle whatever might happen with Micah.

"You wouldn't think he'd bring it here," I say, still unable to get off the topic. "You'd think he wouldn't want it anywhere near him if it has any proof of him killing her. But maybe it doesn't. Maybe it's her phone and nothing more."

I'm suddenly feeling less confident that the phone might be the key we need to get rid of Micah, to prove he killed Rita, to ensure the police take him from our home. If it's just her phone then that's not evidence, is it? It's weird, but not evidence.

"We can ask him," I say. "We can call the police and they can come right over and ask him. We could have an answer right away."

"If he killed her," Ethan says, his eyes still locked on the phone, "you'd think he would have dumped it with her body in the ravine, right? Not brought it here?"

His words wash over me and I freeze, trying to dig deep enough to figure out why what he said doesn't sit right with me.

It's strange to contemplate murdering someone. And what you would do with their phone. It's strange to try to get into a murderer's mindset that way and think it through, but that's not what makes my stomach flip.

"What did you say?" I step back from Ethan, my mind racing. I can't put my finger on what he said. All I know is that there are warning bells going off in my head.

In school, we're taught to pay attention to *funny tummy feelings*, that our bodies might know something is wrong with a situation before we're able to figure it out ourselves. I always thought that was bunk, that there was no way your stomach can tell you anything other than the fact that you're hungry.

But right now my stomach is twisted into knots.

"I said that you would think he'd have dumped the phone in the ravine with her body if he killed her," Ethan says, and now he finally looks up from the phone.

Only now I wish he hadn't. Now I wish he were looking anywhere but at me, because it hit me what he said that made me suddenly feel like I was going to be sick.

The ravine.

The police told me Rita's body was dumped in a ravine, but I didn't tell Micah and I certainly didn't tell Ethan. I didn't want either of them to think about her, once so full of life, twisted and dead, her body left for scavengers in the cold dark.

I know I didn't tell him.

Maybe the police did. Maybe they followed up with him and he forgot to tell me. Maybe, like me, he wanted to spare me that detail so it didn't haunt me in the middle of the night. I search his eyes, looking for any proof that I'm right, that he was protecting me.

Ethan frowns. I swear his eyes darken. He takes a step towards me.

But he never looks away from me.

"Zoe, what's wrong?"

He knows. He knows what happened to Rita.

46

ZOE

"I think we need to call the cops," I say. It's the only thing I can think of to say while my mind tries to grapple with the reality of the situation.

How does Ethan know where Rita's body was found?

"That's not necessary." Ethan glances down at the phone in his hand. "Not right now. You and I can figure this out, right? If we think Micah killed his mom, then we want to know for sure before we get the cops involved." He doesn't look up at me when he speaks.

"Sure." I swallow hard as I stare at my husband. He's still tapping away on the phone, his brow furrowed. "Hey, how did you know the police found her body in a ravine?"

"What?" He sounds distracted and slowly looks up at me from the phone. "You told me."

Not true. Before I can stop myself, I'm speaking. "I didn't."

The look he gives me sends a chill up my spine. The corners of his mouth twitch, like he's fighting back a smile, but what there could be to smile about, I don't know.

"You must have, Zoe. You're so busy you forgot. It

happens to the best of us." He pauses. "Say it. Say you told me."

I take a step back. This can't be happening.

My husband killed Rita. He killed her and dumped her and then pretended he wasn't involved. That's why he didn't want me touching the phone. There has to be something there—maybe calls, maybe texts—something that will tie him to her on the night she disappeared.

And that's why he didn't want Micah here at first, but then what choice did he have? I pushed so hard he couldn't say no and then the boy came to live with us. And then, when I wanted him gone, when I was convinced Micah was the murderer, it was too late.

Ethan sucks in a breath. I swear, his eyes narrow as he stares at me, his gaze so dark, so intense, that I feel like I'm wilting under it.

I know the truth. And he knows I know.

"I'm calling the police," I say, my voice a whisper.

"I don't think that's an option right now." Ethan puts the phone behind him on the counter and crosses his arms. I see how the muscles there twist and bunch. He's strong, much stronger than I am. I don't know if he's standing like this to prove a point, to rub it in my face, or if it's subconscious, but it's clear to me I wouldn't win in a fight.

I have to call the police.

My phone is still in my back pocket and I reach back there, hoping to slide it free. Maybe I can dial it without looking. Isn't there a way you can press the power button a certain number of times in a row and it will call 911? I think I read that somewhere online in a safety article, but I didn't worry about committing it to memory.

That was stupid.

"Give me your phone, Zoe." Ethan sounds tired. He holds out his hand and I freeze. "You don't want me to have to take it from you."

No, I don't. I know how that would go. Slowly, so he can see I'm not trying to pull one over on him, I hand him my phone, then I step back from him.

"Why did you kill her?" I have to know. It's stupid, maybe, to admit that I know the truth, but I can't let him kill me without knowing the truth.

"Rita." His voice is hard as he tosses my phone onto the counter behind him. I always thought he was so handsome in scrubs, like a TV doctor, but now the color of them makes me want to throw up. "She called me, you know. Wanting money."

I can't answer. How would I know this?

"A lot of money. For drugs. She was an addict, Zoe." His voice is hard. Angry. "She was in debt to her dealer and had to pay him back or she was going to be in a lot of trouble. She threatened to tell everyone about Micah, to take me to court for child support. She was going to ruin everything."

"So you killed her?" This is horrifying. I can't even wrap my mind around the fact that this is a conversation I'm having with my husband. "You don't kill someone for that!"

"Did you hear me?" He screams the words in my face. Spittle hits my cheek. "She was going to ruin everything! Everything! Can you imagine what people would say when they found out I had a child with her? She wasn't like this in college, but she was a druggie! Sick! Pathetic! I brought her phone here to keep tabs on her, to make sure people weren't worried about her! Then I left it and you had to find it. You ruined everything!" He pants, then runs his hand through his hair.

I have to fight to keep myself from looking up at the ceiling. Thank God I didn't tell Ethan that Micah is home. I hope the boy is sick enough to sleep through this.

Or maybe he'll hear the commotion. He could get a phone, call the cops... but he has no phone.

A soft whimper escapes my lips.

"I didn't have a choice, Zoe. She forced my hand." He smiles at me, but it's more like he's baring his teeth. "Exactly like you have right now."

"No." The word is a whisper. "No, Ethan. You don't have to do this. I can help you. We can cover this up. We can—"

"Blame Micah?" His words are hard. Cold. "No, you know full well that would never work. They'd catch on. The police might be stupid, but they're not *that* stupid. You're going to have to try harder. You did this, Zoe. You should have left well enough alone."

He's walking towards me and I keep backing up, unable to stop myself from moving away from him. If I can keep some distance between us, if I can somehow manage to keep out of his reach, then I'm sure I'll be fine.

Right?

Yeah, right. Isn't that what every stupid heroine in a horror movie thinks?

My eyes flick around the room as I back up. I'm desperate for something—anything—that I could use as a weapon and potentially keep Ethan away from me. There's a knife block by the stove, but we're moving farther away from that with every step, and I don't think there's any way I could dart past him and grab one.

So, no knife. A rolling pin?

But it's in the drawer, tucked out of the way. Even if I were to get to the drawer, I don't think I'd have time to yank it out and brandish it. Besides, what am I going to do? Even if I got a knife, what would I do? *Stab* my husband? The thought is enough to make me feel sick. Even as he advances on me, a terrifying expression on his face, I know there's no way I'd be able to actually fight him off.

So, what then? I'm hopeless as I look around the kitchen, at the stack of mail I need to go through, the recycling by the garage door, my purse sitting next to it. I have an old thing of pepper spray in there, buried somewhere under a pile of receipts and bits of trash, but I don't even know if it would work anymore.

And then what? Run out the front door? How long would it be before Ethan realized Micah was in the house and went upstairs to get him? As much as I want to get out of here as quickly as possible, I can't leave him here alone, without anyone to help him fight off his dad.

And then the guilt hits. Guilt that Micah was innocent and I thought he was a murderer. Yes, he was creepy. Yes, he made me feel uncomfortable. But he didn't kill his mother.

Ethan did.

"So you, what? Offered to meet up with her and then killed her?" Maybe if I keep him talking I'll be able to think of some way out of my predicament.

Ethan pauses, obviously surprised that I'm talking to him right now instead of looking for a way out of here.

"That's exactly what happened." He frowns at me. "I told her we needed to talk, that she couldn't go around town spreading my secrets like that. But when we met up she told me either I paid up or she ran her mouth." He takes another step towards me. "I had to stop her."

"But killing her?" I keep thinking about what the officer said about Rita's death. I can't help it.

Bruised.

Strangled.

Thrown into a ravine.

"She was going to ruin everything!" His voice rises until he's screaming again. "Just like you are, Zoe! God, you'd think I'd be better at picking them, but apparently I don't know how to find someone who isn't going to ruin everything as soon as I look away from them."

"Please, Ethan." My hands are up in front of my face, trying to beg him to stay away from me while also trying to gain some protection. "Please, you don't want to do this. I know you don't. I'll help you figure out a way out of this. Trust me, there's always a way out."

"No, Zoe, there isn't. Not this time." He almost sounds sad, just a little, and I drop my hands to get a better look at his face.

Movement right behind him catches my attention. For a moment I panic, wondering who Ethan brought home with him and if they're going to help him kill me.

Then I remember I'm not alone.

Micah.

47

ZOE

M icah's by the recycling, his eyes wide, breathing so hard I can see how violently his chest rises and falls.

I watch in horror as he grabs a wine bottle from the recycling. He holds it by the neck, easy, comfortably, like he's done it a hundred times. And maybe he has. His father is a murderer, but I still don't know exactly what kind of a person Micah is.

"Micah," I whisper, and even though I'm sure there's no way Ethan could possibly hear me, he whips around, his face tight, rage pouring off him in waves. I gasp, my hand reaching out, wanting to stop what's going to happen, but it's already set in motion and there isn't anything I can do to stop it.

Micah lunges, a guttural scream ripped from his throat, and brings the wine bottle down on Ethan's head. The crash of glass is loud, followed by a thud as Ethan falls to the floor. Blood pours from where Micah hit him.

"Oh, my God!" I'm pulled to Ethan, wanting to help him,

but I stop myself from dropping to my knees next to him at the last second. This man was going to kill me. He was going to, I'm sure of it. If Micah hadn't snuck downstairs, if he hadn't heard what Ethan was saying...

"He killed my mom!" Micah screams the words. The broken bottle in his hand drips blood and he glances up at me for a moment before he falls on Ethan, raising the bottle over his head, the pointed, jagged edge catching the light before he slams it down, his screaming so loud and so terrible I have to cover my ears and close my eyes.

But even though I'm pressing my hands against my ears as hard as I can, I still hear him. I still hear the way the glass sounds as it punches into Ethan's skin, the way my husband moans, the way Micah's cries slow, change.

He can't possibly be laughing.

I don't want to look but I make myself, opening my eyes a fraction, just enough to see what's going on. Micah's bent over Ethan's body, the broken bottle still in his hand. His arm moves, up and down, up and down, blood everywhere.

It's *everywhere.*

Blood pools out from Ethan's body, a growing pool, blood running along the grout lines in the tile, spreading out faster than I would have thought possible. It's a fine spray in the air, covering Micah's arms, his face, the table. I see it everywhere, splashed on the cupboards behind him, on the fridge, covering Ethan's face so I can't make out his features.

"Micah! Stop!"

He pauses, his arm above his head, his mouth gritted tight, his lips curled up at the corners, and looks up at me. I'm reminded of *Lord of the Flies*, how the boys went completely off the deep end without someone there to guide them and ensure they made the right choices. *But I was here.*

I was supposed to guide him, I was supposed to make sure he knew right from wrong while he was under my roof, because apparently Rita never did.

"You have to stop," I whisper, and I reach out like I'm going to touch him, but then I see the red splashed up on my hand, my arm, and I look down, surprised to see the spatter all over my clothes.

"He killed my mom," Micah says, then stands, still clutching the broken wine bottle.

I can't see the label—it's all red—but I can imagine what bottle it is, how blissful Ethan and I were when drinking it, what it felt like to spend time with my husband while we each enjoyed a glass of wine.

I can't answer him. I can't argue with that.

"And he was going to kill you." Now Micah does let go of the bottle and it slips from his hand, crashing to the kitchen floor.

I wince.

"Don't you see, Mom? He was going to kill you!" His voice gets higher, tighter, louder. "If I wasn't here and I didn't stop him, he was going to kill you."

I can't move. Nothing makes sense. My husband killed Rita? No, I want to push that thought from my head even though I know it's true. He confessed it to me, but accepting it is so hard. It's impossible.

"He wouldn't," I say, but then I remember how he came towards me, his hands outstretched, the anger etched on his face. "Oh, my God, Micah."

"Dad was going to kill you." Micah steps over Ethan's body—his body, not *Ethan*, because my husband is gone and all that's left is his body—and hugs me. "He was going to kill you, Mom. I heard him yelling, heard what he was saying, and I knew I had to come down here. I had to stop him. You know it's true. I'm so sorry."

My arms wrap around him without me realizing that I'm moving. Micah's right. As much as I hate to admit it, if he hadn't been upstairs, if he hadn't snuck downstairs to see what was happening, I'd be dead.

We hug a moment longer, then I push away from him and stagger to my phone. My hands are spotted with blood and I wipe them on the seat of my pants—one of the only places not speckled with Ethan's blood—and I call the police.

The phone rings in my ear and I turn, sagging against the counter. Micah stands still, watching me, his hands flexing at his side like he's trying to resist fight-or-flight mode. He eyes never leave my face as I tell the dispatcher what happened, where we are.

That we're okay. But Ethan isn't.

I hang up after promising them we won't touch anything, then gesture for Micah to follow me outside. Out of the corner of my eye I see a flash of pink on the counter and reach for a moment for Rita's phone.

But what does it matter? The truth is out there. My husband is dead. And now I'm left with the son I didn't want, the one who killed my husband to save me.

The one who thinks I'm such a great mother.

EPILOGUE
ZOE

Wednesday September 13

Micah's in the front yard hanging out with a friend from school.

Yep, that's right, I said *a friend*. My son, the one abandoned by his druggie biological mother, the one who killed his father when he was going to murder me, has a friend. They're playing some card game I don't know, something with made-up creatures like orcs and wizards, but they're both laughing and having a good time, so I'm happy.

Anna wants so badly to go out there and play with her brother, but I told her he needs this time alone with his friend, that he'll play with her later. So she's moping in her room, but little kids generally don't mope for very long, so I'm fully expecting to see her back down here before too long.

But before then I want to make some snacks for Micah

and... George? I think his name is George. Strange how names we think are old-fashioned are coming back into style. I guess some people might say that about *Anna*.

I plant my hands on the counter and lean closer to the window to get a better look at Micah. After Ethan died... after Micah killed him, I guess, I thought for sure he would retreat back into his shell, that he would be so broken we wouldn't be able to come through it on the other side.

Not together. Not as a family.

Because how in the world was I to leave him after he saved me? I wasn't about to kick him out of the house, to tell him he couldn't live with Anna and me. His family was gone and I was all he had left. But I didn't think he'd adjust as well as he has.

Not that there haven't been problems. We were pretty silent through Ethan's funeral. Silent while the cops determined that, yes, Ethan had killed Rita. Her phone was full of texts between the two of them with her begging him for money and him telling her no. Then she threatened him and he finally agreed to meet with her.

On the night he told me he was working late.

On the night she went missing.

Shivering, I run my hands up and down my arms. It was terrible to learn that my husband actually killed someone, but after that, after I knew for sure that Micah wasn't the one who did it, he and I reached out to each other. We're connected now, and while I know we still need to work on our relationship, it's coming.

Therapy helps. I go in the morning when he and Anna are at school, then he goes in the afternoon. His therapist can't tell me what they talk about, and I respect that, but she has told me he tends to sit quietly for most of their session.

She's not worried, though. She thinks he'll open up eventually.

He's been through so much at such a young age.

Anytime I think about Ethan I get incredibly sad, and so I push him out of my mind and grab Micah's backpack from the floor by the kitchen table. He doesn't always eat all of his lunch, and while some of it will need to be thrown away, there might be some I can salvage.

Like a bag of chips. That would be perfect to put out for the boys to munch on while they're playing. I'll get a platter of food together for them.

He's got a ton of books and crumpled up papers in his backpack and I hesitate, considering whether or not he'd be upset at me emptying it out for him. I'll put the books back, of course, and I won't go through his papers without him, but it would be nice if he had a cleaner backpack.

Maybe then he wouldn't lose his homework so often.

He truly loves to be outside. He goes on long walks all the time, usually by himself, exploring the neighborhood. Micah set up a small play area in the back yard, tucked into a grove of trees. I can see a flash of his shirt through the branches from the window if I look really hard, but it's private for him back there.

My therapist said that's healthy. That being outside is good for him. That he could use the alone time with his thoughts, so I make sure Anna never bothers him when he's out there. If it's that good for him then I want to make sure he gets as much alone time out there as he wants.

As I'm thinking, I pull out papers. Smooth them into a pile. Set his books next to them. His lunchbox is crumpled at the bottom of his backpack, a sure sign that any leftovers will be squished beyond recognition, but I pull it out anyway before dropping his backpack on the floor.

It jingles.

"What in the world? That sounded like jewelry." The lunchbox goes on the table and I grab the backpack, flipping it upside down and giving it a little shake.

More jingling, then bits of metal fall from the open zipper, clattering against the table. There are eight or ten of them, all the size of a quarter, but all in different shapes.

A circle. A rectangle. A fish.

A heart.

My fingers tremble as I pick one up to get a better look at it.

Fluffy on one side.

An address and phone number on the back.

No. No, this can't be what I think it is.

I force myself to put it down and look at the others.

Simba.

KitKat.

Tiger.

I close my eyes, squeezing *Tiger* so hard in my fist that I feel the edge of the metal cutting into my palm. In that moment, everything makes sense.

The missing cat posters.

Micah spending so much time alone, outside, hidden from view.

I drop the tag to the table and stumble back to look out the window. Micah's laughing about something, his head thrown back, but I can't hear him. The windows are too good. Sounds outside don't carry in here.

I thought he was saving me from Ethan. He protected me but he didn't go any farther than that, did he?

Remember you thought you saw him smile.

Oh, my God.

I'm gripping the edge of the counter, breathing hard but unable to fully catch my breath. My head pounds as I try to think through what I've just discovered, what it means, who this boy really is.

They say the apple doesn't fall far from the tree.

That a son is just like his father.

And, in this case, I think it might be true.

THANK YOU FOR READING

Did you enjoy reading *The Better Mother*? Please consider leaving a review on Amazon. Your review will help other readers to discover the novel.

ABOUT THE AUTHOR

Emily Shiner always dreamed of becoming an author but first served her time as a banker and a teacher. After a lifetime of devouring stacks of thrillers, she decided to try her hand at writing them herself. Now she gets to live out her dream of writing novels and sharing her stories with people around the world. She lives in the Appalachian Mountains and loves hiking with her husband, daughter, and their two dogs.

ALSO BY EMILY SHINER

The Secret Wife

The Promise

The Caretaker

Her Perfect Life

The Stolen Child

I'm Following You

You Can't Hide

Her Husband's Secret

The Better Mother

Made in the USA
Coppell, TX
23 December 2023

26825852R00146